CALL TO ARMS:

MW00907185

CONSCIENTIOUS OBJECTOR

Colonel Jonathan P. Brazee
USMC (Ret)

Copyright © 2019 Jonathan Brazee

Semper Fi Press

A Semper Fi Press Book

Copyright © 2018 Jonathan Brazee

ISBN-13: 978-1-945743-34-4 (Semper Fi Press)
ISBN-10: 1-945743-34-4

Printed in the United States of America

Acknowledgements:
I want to thank all those who took the time to pre-read this book, catching my mistakes in both content and typing. I want to thank Kelly O'Donnell, James Caplan, and Micky Cocker. Any remaining typos and inaccuracies are solely my fault.

Original Cover Art by Almaz Sharipov

DEDICATION

Dedicated to Corporal Desmond Doss, US Army
Conscientious Objector
Awarded the Medal of Honor for Actions on Okinawa During
WWII

Chapter 1

War came to Capernica on a beautiful Landing Day.

Landing Day had always been Harris' favorite holiday ever since his family arrived as refugees nine years ago, and the celebration at Red Rocks Park, just upstream from the provincial capital of San Isabella, was the largest in the continent. The food, people watching, exhibits, and fireworks show were a good bit of why he loved the holiday, but on a deeper level, it was patriotism. Not every planet welcomed his kind, and he was grateful that they'd found a home.

Life on Capernica wasn't perfect for Assisians, but it was significantly better than what his family had faced on Xander, where they were called parasites and cowards, among the least insulting terms. It wasn't only words. Harris' uncle Theo had been beaten to death by a drunk mob, and that was the final straw and what spurred the family to try and find peace as colonists on Capernica.

"Ooh," his little sister Lynda said as she watched the girl behind the counter dip the stick into the vat where the negatively charged spikes attracted the candy molecules. Within seconds, the candy was swirling around the stick.

"That will be two unis," the young woman behind the counter said, leaning over the counter to hand the little girl the mist-candy.

Harris swiped his wristcomp over the reader, giving the girl a huge smile. She was simply stunning, slender with blue-and-white-streaked hair setting off a heart-shaped face, and her smile made his heart skip a beat. Not that he was going to attempt to get to know her. His family was not keen on interrelations with people from other religions.

At least that was the excuse he gave himself.

"Don't tell mom I gave it to you," he told Lynda.

"Ah, spoiling the little one," the girl said with a laugh.

She looked around to see if anyone was looking, then dipped another stick into the vat and charged it. She glanced around one more time to see if anyone was watching, then leaned over to give it to Lynda.

"Here you go. For later," she said.

Harris was surprised, and he started to swipe his wristcomp again when she reached out to stop him.

"My treat. She reminds me of my little sister."

"Uh . . . thank you," he said flustered. "Lynda, thank the lady."

"Thank you," Lynda said, her face already buried in the mist, her tongue darting in and out as the candy particles swarmed it.

This was one of the reasons he appreciated Capernica. There was a pioneer spirit of everyone watching out for each other, of generosity. In theory, at least. If the girl knew he was an Assisinan, would she be as friendly?

"Are you done?" someone asked from behind him.

Harris turned to see another young woman, this one in the uniform of a Confederation soldier. Shorter than him by a good eight centimeters, she wore the shiny gold bars of a second lieutenant.

"Oh, sorry," he said, stepping back from the counter, pulling Lynda with him.

"Wait," he whispered to Lynda as the little girl started back to where they'd left the family. "Eat up first before mom sees you."

Lynda smiled and nodded, but didn't say anything, her tongue too busy sweeping up the candy particles that whirled around the stick.

Harris looked back up at the soldier. He didn't hate military people. Assisians believed hate was violence in its own right, after all. But he didn't understand them. This woman was only a little older than he was, her short brown hair neatly trimmed at collar-level. Take off the uniform, and she could fit in behind the counter serving mist-candy herself.

What had driven her to join the Army? Why would anyone want to be part of an organization whose very purpose was to kill other human beings?

Yes, there was a war going on, but far, far away from this arm of the sector. Life in Capernica was out of the mainstream, which suited Harris just fine.

"I've got that, Lieutenant," an older man behind the soldier said, reaching around her to swipe his wristcomp. "*Vigilamus pro te.*"

She turned around, obviously surprised, and said, "*Vigilamus pro te.* Thank you, sir."

The old man's weathered face broke into a smile. "I weren't no officer, ma'am. Made master sergeant before I lost this to a pirate in the Avon Sector," he said, lifting his right arm and rapping it on the edge of the counter.

Harris hadn't noticed that the arm was a prosthetic. He frowned. That was just one more piece of proof that war was stupid. Why couldn't people see that?

"You were a grunt?" the female soldier asked.

"Yes, ma'am. Proud of it. And you? Just finish OCS?" he asked, pointing to her chest, which didn't have any of the colored ribbons that Harris had seen before on recruitment ads.

"Logistics school. I'm heading to Interpolative Planning School on Braxton in another week, so I came home for Landing Day. After I graduate and report in to my new unit, I may not be able to come home for the duration."

"Braxton? We've got bases there?" the old man asked.

"Temporary," the lieutenant said. "Some of the schools moved out there from the core what with the war. Uh . . . do you want one?" she asked, lifting her mist-candy.

"No, thanks. I just saw you in line and wanted to pay for it."

"How about a beer then? It would be my honor."

"Now, you're speaking my language, Lieutenant," he said with a smile and held out his prosthetic hand. "Master Sergeant Lester Arceneaux, Army of the Confederation, Retired."

"Second Lieutenant Wysoki," she said, shaking his hand. "Cel Wysoki."

"Come on, Lynda, finish up. Mom's going to be wondering where we are," Harris quietly told his sister, ashamed for having been eavesdropping.

"I'm trying," Lynda said, still chasing the swirling candy particles. "But it keeps getting away from me."

Harris looked at the two soldiers, one new and one old as they stepped away from the mist-candy booth. He had no desire to ever become a soldier. His religion forbade the taking of a life, so what use would he be? More than that, being a soldier was a perversion of humanity. "Thou shalt not kill" was a standard of most religions.

But he felt a pang of regret after the camaraderie he'd just witnessed. Two people, separated by decades, were now heading off to share a beer as if they were long-time friends. Outside of his family, Harris had never felt that kind of connection with anyone. He had acquaintances back in Little Fork, but never any close friends.

The lieutenant was laughing at something the old soldier said when a clap reverberated across the sky, something Harris felt in his bones. Another, then yet another washed over them, and everyone stopped to look up.

It's way too early for the fireworks, Harris told himself as he wondered what was going on.

In the sky to the south over San Isabella, dozens of streaks of smoke had appeared and were heading for the ground.

In the stunned silence, Harris clearly heard the old soldier tell the young one, "You'd better report in, ma'am."

"But I don't have a unit here. I'm on leave."

"I think your leave's been canceled. Unless I miss my guess, those are Wolvic landing craft."

What? Harris wondered as he pulled Lynda close. *Wolvics? They aren't supposed to be this far out.*

He picked up Lynda and started pushing through the crowd. If the old soldier was right, he had to get to his family and get back home before all hell broke loose. Given the man's obvious experience, Harris was leaning to give him the benefit of the doubt.

He wasn't as sure, however, as he made his way back to the pavilion where he'd left his family. Most of the people were standing around, watching the aerial show and pointing with "oohs" and "ahs." More and more ships were appearing, but from the tiny bits and pieces of conversations he heard, it seemed that people thought it was the Capernica Air Force putting on a show for Landing Day.

"Mom, we've got to leave," he said as he reached their table.

She gave him a perplexed look from where she was feeding his father. "It's still early. No reason to rush."

"Now, Mom. Please don't argue," he urged as he sat Lynda down on the table and started to take off his father's bib.

"What's gotten into you, Harris?" she asked, reaching to put the bib back on. "He's not finished with his lunch."

"Look up in the sky," he said quietly, grabbing her hand.

The pavilion didn't have walls, but it was covered. Harris' mother wrinkled her brows and asked, "What do you want me to look at?" as she made her way past the other picnic tables and out from under the roof.

She looked up, and her mouth dropped open. A flash lit up the inside of the pavilion, and several people started clapping.

Harris wiped his father's face and stood him up before looking around until he spotted his sister outside the pavilion, watching the sky along with everyone else, with Regis, their younger brother, in tow.

"Kate, come here!" he shouted.

"Where's Mom?" she asked as she made her way through the tables to him. "You need help with Dad?"

"We're leaving. Help me pack this stuff up."

"Leaving? No way! I told you, I'm meeting Su-Min and some of the others—"

"We're leaving. Now. Don't argue!"

"You're not my boss. You can leave, but I'm not—"

Harris grabbed her hand and held it tightly. "We have to leave now," he said as his mother returned.

"What's going on, Harris?" she asked.

"That's just the Air Force putting on a show," Kate said dismissively.

Harris looked around to see if anyone was listening, then quietly said, "Those might be Wolvics."

"Wolvics?" his sister said. "What would they—"

"Shhh!" he interrupted, putting his hand over her mouth.

"Are you sure they're Wolvics?" his mother asked, her face gone pale.

"No, but a soldier is. I heard him. We need to go before there's a panic. If there is . . ." he said, nodding his head at his father.

Warden Tayman had started his family late in life, but he still should be a hearty and hale man. There were some rare neurological conditions, however, that were still beyond the help of modern medicine, and his father had faded quickly over the last year. Harris didn't know how much of his father, if any, was still inside that once quick-witted mind. He'd react to gentle commands, but there was no way they could get him to the docks if there was a panic-fueled mob rushing for the river buses.

"Now, Kate. We're going," Harris' mother said, coming to the same conclusion. "Keep ahold of Regis."

She swept up their lunch into the backpack and gave it to Harris. She helped her husband up, and with one arm firmly wrapped around his, she led him out of the pavilion and headed for the docks.

They weren't the only ones leaving. Most of the people were watching the sky, others had gone back to whatever they were doing before, but there was already a small exodus of worried-looking people making their way either to the riverside or to the parking lots. Harris put Lynda on his shoulders and led the way for his mother and father while Kate and Regis brought up the rear. Keeping tight, they managed to stay together.

As they reached the slope leading down to the docks, Harris let out a sigh of relief. He still wasn't sure that the old soldier had been right, but better safe than sorry. He paused to take a look back when a single spaceplane approached the park from the activity toward the south. It streaked at an unbelievably high rate of speed, coming in low. As it reached the park, it popped up and gained altitude, to the cheers of thousands.

A wave of foreboding swept over Harris, and he started to urge his mother to speed up when a fireball erupted over the midway. The Ferris wheel and the Mad Chute, the two tallest rides, disintegrated. A moment later, a concussion wave swept over them

Cheers turned to cries of fear, almost immediately followed by thousands of wristcomps going off with a general alert ordering all citizens to return to their homes and await further instructions.

The slow exodus to the docks turned to a mad rush as people surged forward.

"Stick with me!" Harris shouted as Lynda clutched his head in fear, her little hands covering his eyes.

He reached back to grab his father's free hand and pull him forward, but his father resisted. He only had one pace anymore, and that was slow.

"Push him, Mom. We've got to get to the bus."

Bodies jostled them in the melee. Harris looked back, and a tsunami of people was forming as what had happened sunk in, and they started to flee. There were more options on this side of the river, but for those on the eastern banks, it was the river buses or heading down to San Isabella to try the bridge—San Isabella over which it was now obvious that the Wolvics were attacking.

Someone shouldered Harris hard, almost knocking Lynda off his shoulder. He had to release his father to grab ahold of her and keep her up. If she went to the ground, she'd be trampled.

People surged past them, and up ahead, he could see people already boarding the northbound bus. It was a Blue-Line with a capacity of 176 people. Running on automatic, once that number was reached, it would leave the dock.

If many more people passed them, the Tayman family was not going to make it.

Harris turned to his mother and handed her Lynda and his backpack. He swung himself around, squatted down, offering his back, and grabbed his father's thighs. By some miracle, his father seemed to understand, and he wrapped his arms around Harris' neck.

He stood and shouted, "Now run!"

His father might not be mentally there anymore, but his body had not gotten smaller. Harris grunted as he tried to run with his father's weight bearing him down. Other people jostled him, and each time, he started losing his grip. His father started sliding, but he refused to give up. His eyes were glued to the ramp, and nothing else mattered. He reached the path leading down to the docks, and he slowed to a walk, but he wasn't in the clear yet. He tried to estimate a count, but his arms were screaming, his lungs were heaving too much for his mind to make sense of the mass of people.

"Out of my way!" someone shouted from behind, and Harris felt his mother push up against him, almost knocking him over.

"Back off!" Kate screamed. "Stop pushing."

"Mom, slip past me," he said, turning half-way around.

With Lynda crying in her arms, she sidled past him, followed by Kate and Regis. An older man, his face flushed red, tried to follow Kate, but Harris stepped back out. The man pushed against him, but Harris wasn't going to let him past.

Asissians didn't believe in the taking of life, but they'd been oppressed enough over the ages that they'd learned passive resistance. Harris was not going to let this jerk by.

The man kept up a string of curses, but Harris ignored him, shifting to cut him off as they edged down the stairs to the gangway. His father was getting heavier and heavier, and Harris was losing his grip, but he just needed to hang on a little longer.

What am I doing?

They were no longer running, so he didn't have to carry his father. Harris slowly let him slide down until he was on his own two feet. He interlocked his right arm with his father's left. Nothing was going to make his father hurry faster than he wanted, so with the two of them, they'd created a rolling roadblock. The man behind them could curse all he wanted, but he was not getting by.

Harris kept watching those boarding. A tally was kept at the head of the gangway: 156 . . . 157 . . . 158. He couldn't get an accurate count of how many were in front of him, but it would be close.

Please, let us get aboard.

It wasn't exactly a prayer. Asissinans didn't believe in prayer for personal gain. If Harris and his family made it aboard, then that meant six others would not and would have to wait. Still, he could give thought to his hopes.

And then his mother and Lynda passed the gate, then Kate and Regis.

The light flashed 173 and 174 as Harris and his father stepped onto the gangway. Harris let out a huge sigh of relief.

The man who'd been pushing behind them made it on as well, so all his bluster had been for nothing.

The gate chimed and closed as the last person passed it, to the cries and shouts of those still trying to board. Harris stepped onto the deck of the bus before he turned around. The red-faced man got into his face and yelled something, but Harris tuned him out. His attention was on the shore, where thousands of people were pushing and shoving to get down to the docks.

If it hadn't been for the old soldier, Harris and his family would be in that mass of people. He muttered a quick prayer for their safety, but he didn't feel guilty at being relieved that he and his family had made it.

Chapter 2

With the river bus at capacity, it pulled out into the current. Once clear, the repeller jets kicked in, lifting the hull as the bus picked up speed. To the south, smoke was gathering over San Isabella. Smoke also rose over Red Rock. Some people watched silently, mouths open in shock, while others congregated to discuss what was going on.

Harris gathered his family into the bow where they managed to grab a spot on the bench for his father and the two little ones. He stood protectively in front of them, his mother and sister at his side.

Ten minutes into the voyage, people screamed in fear as one, then another jet flew low past them, the river water kicked up into a mist by their fanjets until someone shouted out they were Militia Air Force. Screams turned into cheers. Harris watched as the fighters streaked south, barely clearing the water.

Harris knew the fighters were on their way to kill fellow human beings, and while the thought repulsed him, there was still a little stirring of pride and excitement . . . and that made him feel guilty. Human life was human life, whether Capernican or Wolvic.

"There they go," someone said as the now-distant fighters popped up, reaching for altitude before turning again to swoop down on the capital.

"Get the bastards!" a woman shouted beside Harris, her voice full of venom.

People joined in to cheer, but the cheers turned to groans when fingers of light reached out, flaring around both fighters until they came apart in midair. Harris felt his heart stop. He'd just watched two human beings being killed. It was unfathomable, but there it was.

A pall came over the passengers as it really began to sink in. People exchanged worried looks with each other. This was real, not some holovid.

It hit Harris as well. Everything had been so rushed from the moment he'd heard what the old soldier had said until now, but how he felt . . . helpless?

Lynda was softly crying, and that was something he could address. He picked up his little sister and held her against his chest, patting her back. He had to be the strong one here.

If there was ever a time when Harris wished his father was the same vibrant man who'd brought the family to Capernica, now was it. But his father sat on his seat, his green eyes, once so vivid and full of intelligence, now dull and lifeless, his hand tightly holding on to his wife's.

Lynda twisted to face Harris, tears still glistening on her cheeks, and held out one of the mist-candy sticks that she'd somehow managed to retain throughout the struggle to get onto the river bus. The power was depleted, whatever candy particles she hadn't managed to scarf down fallen to the floor.

"Don't worry, little one," he said. "Three stops, and we're home. I'll see what we can get you then."

Chapter 3

The next three days were spent trying to follow the news. The Wolvics had landed in force all over the planet. The Capernican militia, such as it was, was being pushed back. The question on everyone's mind was when the Confederation Army would arrive. There was a small permanent Army garrison in Miguel Pass, but it would take several Army divisions to push back the invaders, from all accounts.

The problem was that the Confed Army and Navy were heavily engaged, not only with the Wolvics, but with their Truth Seeker and Triple W allies—and far from this sector. The Wolvics were making a bold move to hold Capernica, either as a bargaining chip or to keep whenever the current hostilities came to a close.

Immediately after the invasion, twenty-one of Little Fork's young men and women had left to go fight the invaders. Wristcomps now worked only intermittently, but word did make it back that six of them had been killed in combat already. Harris wasn't exactly friends with any of them, but he knew them all, and news of their loss hit him hard.

Forest Popovic, the closest that Harris could call a friend, had been one of the people to volunteer. He'd asked Harris to come with him, but he'd refused, reminding his friend that he was an Assisian. Forest had blown up at that, saying that things were different now that they'd been invaded. Harris had remained firm, and in the end, Forest had stormed out of their home, saying he could no longer be friends with a coward.

Harris cried that night in bed, but he didn't know if that was in concern for Forest's safety or in sadness for his own loss.

The family spent most of the time at home, staying out of the way. The holovid feed was cut off, so he and Kate spent time reading to the young ones while they waited for more snippets of news that were packet-delivered whenever there was an opening in the ethersphere.

The third morning after the invasion dawned sunny and warm. After a large breakfast of pancakes and Johnson strips, the family settled into the living room. His father soon fell asleep, and his snores prompted giggles from Lynda and Regis.

Lynda gave her favorite book, *Asi and the Elephant*, to Harris and crawled into his lap. Before he'd gotten halfway through, however, she was asleep, too, her tiny snores a tiny reflection of her father's.

With Lynda asleep on his lap, Harris' eyes were beginning to droop when his wristcomp general alarm jerked him awake. Everyone's alarms were going off, and Lynda started crying.

It wasn't yet another report of territory loss. It was a command to head to the middle school for an announcement. Harris didn't know what couldn't just be passed on the network, and he contemplated hanging back. Assisians were often not trusted even in good times, and he'd already heard a few snide comments, including JohnJohn Morrisey, who loudly whispered—purposely loud enough for Harris to hear—that they might be spies. He really didn't want to be mixing with the rest of the village. But Assisians also preached fealty to the government, and this message was coming over the A-Band.

With his mother assisting his father, he and Kate got Lynda and Regis ready. Within ten minutes, they left their home, with Harris making sure to lock the doors, something that normally wasn't necessary in Little Fork. They joined the general mass of people as they made their way down to River Road and Giada Huhn Middle School.

Harris held Lynda on his hip as he surveyed the crowd. It looked like the entire village had turned out. But for what? Millie Tenter, Little Fork's provost, was huddled up with some of the town's movers-and-shakers, but she didn't look like she'd be running whatever this was.

"Any idea what' going on?" Lisa Heindrich asked, two-year-old Frankie on her hip, matching him and Lynda.

"Not a clue," Harris said. "Hopefully, they'll tell us soon."

Lisa was one of his schoolmates and lived next door to him. They were on friendly, if not close terms. She'd had Frankie at 17, the first in his age group to have a child, but had never revealed who the father was. Harris was curious, as were most of his ex-schoolmates, but it didn't affect him one way or the other. If she didn't want to share that with anyone, it was her choice.

An approaching vehicle coming up River Road caught everyone's attention, and all talking ceased. The hover was a dull olive green, with a white and red Confederation logo on the hood, but other than that, it looked like a normal passenger hover, the kind anyone could buy at the dealer across the river in Fox. It was hard to tell with the paint job and what looked to be custom lights, but Harris thought it might be a Jepson Gazelle.

It pulled to a stop, and three soldiers got out. They were wearing full battle gear, which looked a little discordant getting out of a Gazelle. The crowd parted as they made their way to the school entrance.

One of them stepped to the front, turned on his throat mic, then said, "I am Master Sergeant Koppleman of the Confederation Army. This is Sergeant Lin, and that is Corporal Synx."

The man's accent was inner arm, so he was a long way from home.

"We are from Camp Lassiter," which Harris knew was the official name for the garrison at Miguel Pass. "And as of now, we are here to defend Little Fork from the Wolvic invasion."

There was a sudden outbreak of muttering from the crowd.

"Just you three?" Def Mortenson shouted out. "Where's the rest of the army?"

Mr. Mortenson could be an obnoxious loudmouth, but this time, he was only voicing what was on everyone else's mind.

"I'll get to that," the soldier said. "But first, we've got the formalities. As you all know by now, the Wolvics have landed in force on the planet. San Isabella, White Water,

Warrenton, and New Leeds have all fallen, and Pryce is under siege."

There were gasps from the crowd. That meant four of the six provincial capitals had been captured, and the planet's capital was being attacked. Harris knew things were not going well, but to this extent still shocked him.

"Accordingly," the soldier continued, "under the approval of the Council Prime, and as allowed under Paragraph two-point-three-point-two of the Articles of Confederation, Capernica is now under Martial Law, Level One." He pulled out a small pad, and pressed the screen.

Immediately, Harris' wristcomp—and what sounded like everyone's wristcomp—alerted.

"You all should now have a copy of the Declaration of Martial Law: Three-Six-Six-Three-One. It will take effect—" he started until one of the other soldiers leaned in and said something to him. He looked at his wristcomp, then said, "It already took effect five minutes ago."

Harris barely glanced at his wristcomp. It would be full of government legalese. What he wanted to know was how it was going to affect the village.

"Now, to answer the gentleman's question, the garrison is heavily engaged with the Wolvics, and we do not expect relief from other Confed forces in the near term."

"Where does that leave us? How are three of you going to protect us?" someone shouted out.

The soldier smiled, but Harris didn't think it was a very friendly smile.

"I am here with two primary missions at the moment. The first is to prepare your village for evacuation," he said to the cries of the crowd. He stood there, holding up his hand for silence. It took a while, but the noise subsided. "San Isabella has fallen. Our Intel believes those forces will start moving upriver, clearing all of the towns along the way.

"We need to be prepared for that. If they start moving north, you need to be ready to evacuate to the cave systems in the hills surrounding you. If they don't come or are somehow defeated before that, then the evacuation order will never take place."

"What's the second mission?" Mr. Mortenson shouted out.

"Twenty-one of your brave citizens have already joined in the defense of the planet, protecting others. I am here to conscript another thirty-three to serve in the Planetary militia to protect your own village. With the three of us leading you, this will be Little Fork's defense. Please stand by for the names of those of you selected."

There were murmurs from the crowd, but many had expressed their belief over the last three days that this might be coming down the pike. Thirty-three more would be a big chunk to absorb for such a small village. Harris looked around, trying to gauge how many people of military age were left.

At least I don't have to worry about that. I'll help with this evacuation plan, but I don't have to fight.

The same Articles of Confederation that the soldier had quoted gave religious protection to conscientious objectors. He couldn't be forced into uniform.

"Wait!" Ms. Thames, the third and fourth-grade teacher said, stepping out. "I'm volunteering to serve."

Harris turned to look at the soldier, wondering what he'd say. Ms. Thames was in her mid-forties, not someone Harris imagined in uniform.

"Very well," the soldier said after a moment. "Give your name to Corporal Synx. Anyone else?"

Ten more people raised their hands and stepped forward. Harris knew that two of them were only 15 or 16, friends of Kate, but no one said anything. Harris thought about stepping up and outing them, but he held back.

"Sergeant Lin, read out the names. The original list," he said as the ten volunteers were being recorded into the system. "Everyone else, please stay put. For those of you called out, you'll be able to go home and get ready. Come back with sturdy footwear and trousers. We've got uniform tops. Be back here in an hour."

One of the soldiers, a short, broad-shouldered man stepped forward, looking at his pad.

"The first group will form First Squad, under command of Master Sergeant Koppleman. Raise your hand when I call your name."

This soldier had an even stronger inner arm accent than the first one. Another foreigner.

"Erin Blaystone," he announced.

Erin was in her mid-thirties. The mother of three, her husband Brand was one of the volunteers who'd left the day of the invasion. Harris frowned. They were starting pretty old, he thought, and they'd have to let Erin off. Who else would take care of the kids?

The soldier called off ten more names, ranging from Erin to young Bill Leung, a 17-year-old high school senior. Jared Grant was called, but he was one of those who had just volunteered. Some of them pumped the air with their fists when they heard their name, some merely shrugged, and some looked pensive.

"Time's a'wasting," the master sergeant called out. "You've got 60 minutes to be back here, ready to go."

The soldier—the sergeant—called out another ten names, all of them going to Second Squad. This time, four were among those who'd volunteered. There were no other surprises, but the pool of potentials was getting smaller. Lynda squirmed in his grasp, wanting down.

"Hold on, Pumpkin. Let them finish so we can go back home," he whispered to her.

"Now, the final twelve. You'll be with me and Third Squad. Raise your hand so I can see you.

"Lisa Heindrich."

Beside him, Lisa slumped ever-so-slightly, then raised her free hand.

"Sorry about that, Lisa," he whispered.

"No, someone has to do it, Harris. This is our home."

"What about Frankie?"

"This is his home, too. I'll just ask my mom to look after him while I'm gone."

"Johnjohn . . . uh, is that right?" the sergeant asked, looking around in confusion. "Johnjohn Morrisey?"

Johnjohn gave a shout and pummeled the air while his younger brother slapped him on his back.

Harris raised his eyebrows. Johnjohn was a year older than him, and he'd been one of the boys who'd made life rough for the eleven-year-old new kid in town. The local kids had been delighted to find someone who wouldn't fight back, no matter the provocation, and he'd been beaten up too many times before they finally tired of their bullying. He and Johnjohn weren't on bad terms now, but they weren't on friendly terms, either.

"Addad McMoud."

Harris didn't really know the river bus captain. Ten years older than him at least, the man spent most of his time ranging the river from San Isabella all the way to Raging Gorge and back again.

"Harris Taymon."

Harris' mouth fell open in shock. There had to be a mistake.

"Taymon, Harris. Raise your hand, man," the sergeant said.

Lisa elbowed him, and he instinctively raised it.

"There, that's not so difficult an order to follow, right?" the sergeant asked to the chuckles of the crowd.

Harris turned around to look at his mother, but his father's eyes caught his attention. There was something in them, as if he understood what was happening.

"Harris," he mouthed.

"Harris," Kate said, running up to him, dragging Regis. "You can't be in the Army."

Mrs. Reimeister, an 80s-something woman living with her son heard Kate and wrinkled her lip in disgust before turning away.

"Don't worry. I'll take care of this."

The sergeant finished with Safer d'Amay and told them they also had just sixty minutes to get back. Harris ignored him. He needed to talk to the man in charge. With Lynda still on his hip, he made his way through the dispersing crowd to where the master sergeant was reading a pad.

"Sir?" he asked when the man acknowledged him.

He almost wished he still hadn't when he looked up, disdain reeking from his eyes.

"Sir, I'm Harris Tayman, and that sergeant called my name—"

"Then I suggest you better get home and take care of your affairs, son."

"No, you don't understand. There's been a mistake."

"The mistake was when the Wolvics thought they could take this planet. With citizens like you, we're going to teach them the error of their ways."

The words were there, but there was no conviction to them. Harris realized that this soldier was not happy with his assignment.

He shook his head to clear it. It didn't matter if the man wasn't happy.

"I mean, I can't be in the Army. I'm a conscientious objector. My whole family is," he said, jiggling Lynda for emphasis.

If he thought the master sergeant had little regard for him before, that had grown into intense animosity. The soldier beamed hate at him, strong enough to score his soul.

"Uh . . . the Articles of Confederation protects my right—"

"Did you hear what I told all you people? You're under Martial Law One, and that supersedes individual rights. So, I tell you what you're going to do. You're going to forget about your conscientious objector claim," he said, spitting venom with the term, "and you're going to be back here so Sergeant Lin can somehow mold you into something that can help defend this village. *Your* village."

Harris gaped at him like a goldfish, shocked. This wasn't how the world worked. People might look down upon Assisians, but they were still protected by the Articles. No one could just . . . *ignore* the Articles!

Anger filled him, and he leaned into the older man, his face centimeters from the soldier's nose, and spit out, "No, I won't. I will not kill another human being."

The soldier stared back at Harris for a long moment, looking deep into Harris' eyes before he calmly said, "Put down your daughter."

That wasn't what Harris was expecting him to say. He turned to look at Lynda, who reached up to touch the side of his face.

"Down," she said, echoing the master sergeant's word.

"She's my sister," he said, confused.

"Then put your sister down."

"Why?"

The master sergeant almost casually removed his sidearm from the holster at his belt, made a show of examining it, then raised it to aim right at Harris' head.

"Because, she's an innocent, and I'm here to protect the innocent. I don't want to hurt her when I blow off your goddamned head!"

"What? You can't do that," Harris sputtered, fear replacing anger.

"Oh, but I can. And I will. Under Martial Law, I am the law here, and I can do whatever I want," he said in a quietly scary voice. "So, what's it going to be? Are you going to be here in another fifty-five minutes, ready to go, or am I going to blow your brains all over this nice lawn?"

People were watching, some shocked, a few with looks of enjoyment. Harris knew that none of them would come to help him, even if they wanted to. And from the looks of it, not many would fall into that category.

"Well, son?" the sergeant asked, his finger making a scritching sound as his index finger stroked the body of his handgun. "What will it be?"

It was hard to break his focus on that sound, but he had to say something. Nothing Saint Francis had taught would compel him to let the soldier kill him. He could agree, and as long as he didn't kill anyone, he could be true to his beliefs. They could put him in a fight, but they couldn't make him kill.

"I'll be back like you said," he managed to choke out, grateful for any lifeline.

The soldier lowered and holstered his weapon. He smiled and said, "I thought so. You've got fifty minutes."

Harris looked around at the others, embarrassed and ashamed. Then he saw his mother, looking at him with a disappointed look. That hurt worse. Hopefully, she'd understand that he wasn't rejecting their religion. They might give him a gun, but he was not going to kill.

"Now don't you have any ideas of sneaking off, son," the soldier said matter-of-factly. "We execute deserters. Maybe their family, too."

Martial Law or not, Harris didn't think the soldier had the authority to do anything to his family. But he wasn't going to push it.

"I'll be back, sir," he said as he rushed through the crowd to get home.

Chapter 4

"You fucking coward. Fire your goddamned weapon, Tayman, or I swear I'll put a round through your worthless head myself," Sergeant Lin screamed, his face red with rage.

Private Harris Tayman, newly of the Capernican Militia Self-Defense Force, lifted his face from the dirt and stared at the sergeant. The muzzle of the man's Bamberger looked huge as it pointed at him, and he knew for a certainty that the sergeant was serious. If Harris didn't do something, he was a dead man.

Harris didn't want to die. Just two months past his 19th birthday, there was too much life in front of him, life that shouldn't be snatched away, not like this.

Rounds stitched the top of the dirt berm behind which gave the squad a modicum of cover, raining clods down on him and making the sergeant dive for the ground. It wasn't just the sergeant who posed a threat to Harris. Down the hill, the Wolvic invaders were doing their best to wipe the Capernican colonists off the planet so they could take ownership. Illegal, but might makes right.

"Now, Tayman," the sergeant hissed, waving the muzzle of his rifle for emphasis.

Gentle Lord, how am I in this position? Help me to see the way, he prayed closing his eyes.

The blast from the sergeant's Bamberger shocked his eyes back open, that and the dirt that splattered his face.

"The next one takes off your fucking head," the sergeant told him.

Is that the answer, Lord?

He didn't know if it was or not, but his body was already moving. He wormed past the body of Landon de Ceer. Landon, who he'd known since their families joined the fifth wave of colonists nine years before. Landon, a fellow conscript who'd been "recruited" along with him three days ago. Landon, who had taken a round through the top of his head at first contact with the enemy.

Harris tried not to look at Landon's face as he edged up to the top of the berm. It was easier, far easier to look down the hill to where the Wolvics were slowly and inexorably making their way to the squad's position.

They didn't look like death, was all Harris could think. Just bodies, rushing from one tiny piece of cover to the next, like children playing "Where am I?" on a lazy summer afternoon.

The staccato of fire from his left made him flinch. Sergeant Lin had taken his position again and was spraying the slope with this Bamberger. He hadn't forgotten Harris, though.

"Next clip is for you, Tayman, if you don't get into the fight."

Harris pulled his ancient Brady .288 up and rested the forestock on the edge of the berm. He looked through the scope as the crosshairs sought out targets, then the rifle's microgyros pressed against his hands, trying to guide him to his aim point.

It felt like the devil itself was trying to take control over him, and he felt despoiled. This was not how humanity was supposed to be.

Harris might have to fire to save his life, but he couldn't do that at the cost of another life, even that of a Wolvic invader. He fought the aiming gyros, forcing his crosshairs high before he pressed the thumb trigger. Nothing happened.

Panic swept over him, and he started to yell out to the sergeant that he was trying before he remembered the safety. The thumb trigger was a small button on the side of the stock, easy to press, even if it was unintended. To keep from accidental discharges, the Brady had a recessed safety. Harris depressed the safety and then hit the trigger again.

His first round left his weapon with barely any recoil, which seemed obscene to him. Dealing death shouldn't be that easy. It should feel consequential.

Not that Harris was going to kill anyone. Every round he fired was high, a mere facade to keep the sergeant from carrying out this threat. Maybe his firing would help dissuade the Wolvics. If that happened, all to the good. But nothing was going to make him take a human life, even if that should cost him his own.

He fired over a dark figure. A moment later, the Wolvic stumbled and fell. He didn't get back up.

Did I do that? Harris wondered, aghast.

He pulled his Brady back and peered down the slope, willing the soldier to get to his feet.

"Harris!" Johnjohn hissed from the next position down the line. "You heard the sergeant. You'd better get into it right now!"

No, I didn't hit him. Someone else did, he thought, doing a good job of convincing himself.

He brought his rifle to bear again, but this time, he added a few extra meters in elevation.

Harris flinched when a trail of fire flashed in front of him, and he ducked back down for cover. But Third Squad wasn't the target. An explosion rocked Second Squad's position, and Harris felt a guilty flood of relief. He didn't want to die this afternoon, but neither did he want the others to die. He knew them, just as he knew everyone in First Squad. It was wrong to feel joy that he hadn't been targeted when others might have just been killed.

"Sergeant, should we retreat?" Georg shouted out. "They're almost here."

"If you do, Handle, I'll cut you down, that's if the Wolvics don't get you first. You just hold on and keep putting rounds downrange," the sergeant snarled.

"But they're not going down," Georg protested. "Their armor is too good."

"Not that good," the sergeant said, changing his point of aim, then firing his big Bamberger.

An instant later, a Wolvic invader fell bonelessly back down the hill, his body sliding a good ten meters before it came to a stop.

Harris felt a quick burst of relief before 19 years of doctrine washed over him in a guilty wave. That soldier the sergeant had just killed was a human being, and all life was precious.

"One less Wolvic motherfucker," the sergeant said with a sneer. "Now all of you, keep up the pressure."

"He's got the Bamberger, and all we've got are these shitty Bradies," Johnjohn muttered before firing another burst down the hill.

Harris turned his head to look behind him. The back side of the ridge sloped precipitously all the way down to Morales Creek, hidden in the trees far below. Harris had spent many warm afternoons exploring the creek, and he was sure if he could get down to it, he could fade away into the wilderness, out of reach of Sergeant Lin and the militia.

He turned to look at the sergeant. The man was firing measured shot after measured shot, intent on the enemy, but he was a coiled spring. Harris didn't know if he could get far enough down the slope to reach cover before the sergeant could target him.

As if he could read Harris' thoughts, the sergeant stopped firing for a moment and looked down the squad line.

"We've got air in thirty seconds. Get your asses down and kiss the dirt," he shouted out.

Harris didn't hesitate. He dropped back down and curled into a fetal ball.

Those were the longest 30 seconds of his life. Twice, he was showered with dirt as Wolvic rounds impacted the top of the ridgeline.

The muffled whisper of a fanjet broke through the firing. Harris looked up in time to glimpse the planetary Air Guard plane as it streaked in spitting death. This wasn't one of the Confederation Navy or Army's top-of-the-line fighters, but Harris couldn't imagine something deadlier. In an instant it was gone.

"Now!" Sergeant Lin shouted. "Fire! Drive them back!"

Harris crawled back up and looked over the ridgeline. To his surprise, Wolvics, some only 50 meters away, were getting up and retreating back down the hill. One stumbled and fell, but he got back up and continued in his retreat.

Around him, the members of his squad fired on the figures, keeping it up until the last one slipped away from view.

Johnjohn stood and started gyrating in a weird dance as he screamed after them, "That's right, you freaks. You came after us, and we kicked your asses."

"Get down, Morrisey," Sergeant Lin ordered. "You looking to eat a round?"

"But we beat them, Sergeant. Kicked their asses."

"We didn't do shit. It was your Air Guard plane. Pretty ballsy of the pilot in that old-tech piece of crap."

"But we held them off until then, right?" Johnjohn persisted.

"Held off a probe, maybe. That weren't no fucking assault. Did you see supporting arms with them? No, that were jus' scouts, probing our lines, feeling us out. Not a real effort. So, get the fuck back down and stop acting like a fool."

Not a real effort? Harris wondered, looking at Landon's body. *Landon's dead, whether that was a "real effort" or not.*

Chapter 5

"What the hell was wrong with you back there," Lisa asked him as they struggled to carry Landon's body back off the line. "I thought the sergeant was going to kill you himself."

Landon was heavy, far too heavy. Harris had his arms under Landon's while Lisa was carrying him at the knees. Blood and brain matter covered Harris' chest. Harris tried to block that out of his mind.

"You know I'm an Assisian," Harris said, hitching Landon up so he could get a better grip, blood making his hands slippery.

"Yeah, but to get your ass killed for that? I mean, the Wolvics invaded us, so you're only protecting yourself. And your family. You can't do that?"

"Not if I have to kill someone myself. It's a sin against God."

Lisa rolled her eyes and said, "Isn't it a sin to commit suicide, too? That's what you'd be doing if you let that sergeant shoot you."

"That's between him and his maker," Harris said.

"That's ridiculous, if you ask me. You can't let people walk over you, and if they're trying to kill you, you gotta take action.

"Look, I don't want to be here any more than you do. No training, an asshole Army regular now with complete control over me. But sometimes life doesn't cooperate with what's good and right. The Wolvics want to take our planet, and they want us gone. I've got my Frankie to protect, and if I have to kill every one of those Wolvic assholes, I'll do it without shedding a tear."

Harris understood her. Lisa's Frankie was two years old, and humans had evolved to protect their young. But did that give her the right to kill someone else? Every other person in the squad would say yes. Even he might, he had to admit to himself, if he had a child to protect.

But where do you draw the line? If protecting a child justifies taking a human life, then did protecting yourself? Protecting your property? Because someone insulted you? No, the line has to be in the taking of human life.

"You need to think on that, Harris. You've got family, too. And us. If you were putting out some fire, maybe Landon would still be here with us," she said, more than a trace of bitterness tinging her voice.

Harris scowled, not at her tone, but because he'd wondered the same thing . . . and he was wracked with guilt. Sergeant Lin had assigned them each into battle buddy teams, where one was supposed to look out for the other. At first contact, Landon had fought while he'd turned his back, refusing to engage the enemy. And now, he was helping carry Landon's body to the platoon collection point.

They carried the body the rest of the way in silence.

****

Harris and Lisa rejoined the squad. The front of his uniform was sticky with drying blood, and he'd been tempted to chuck it, but the sergeant had lectured them back when he'd issued them that first hour that the blouse was the only thing that designated them as "legal combatants." It had something to do with them being in a uniform, which made little sense to him. They were wearing the same trousers they'd had on when the Army team had marched into Little Fork and swept up the 36 new "recruits" three days ago.

Harris sat down, back against the berm as he pulled out his knife to try and scrape off some of the blood. Rainer Lent scowled, stood, and moved several meters away, muttering, "Damned coward." Ivy Kim stood over him for a long moment, not saying a word, then spit on Harris before going to sit beside the others. Ivy's brother had volunteered for the service the day the invaders landed, and he'd been killed two days later outside of New Sandston. Only 16, she'd lied to Sergeant Lin and the other two soldiers in order to join the village militia, and no one had the heart to rat her out.

Harris refused to acknowledge either of them. After 19 years on Xander and Capernica, he was used to it, and he'd been raised to turn the other cheek.

"Tayman, come here," Sergeant Lin growled.

Harris had to fight the urge to roll his eyes. He stood up and started over to where the sergeant was sitting, when the man yelled, "And take your goddamned weapon with you!"

He retreated the few steps, picked up his Brady, and approached the NCO who stood up and motioned for Harris to follow him. The sergeant strode down the back slope of the ridge like a mountain goat, each step sure, while Harris half-slid, half-stumbled after him. They reached the first of the trees when the sergeant spun around, grabbed the taller Harris by the throat, then threw him back against a tree trunk.

Six centimeters shorter than Harris, the broad-shouldered soldier easily out-massed him by thirty kilos. With his air being cut off, Harris knew the man could kill him right here, and no one would blink an eye. Just one more casualty in a senseless war.

He dropped his weapon and grabbed the sergeant's hand, attempting to pull it off his throat, but the man's arm was like steel. His vision started to gray out as the sergeant leaned in, almost nose to nose.

"What the fuck is your problem, Tayman? Are you a coward?" he asked, seemingly sincere, as if he couldn't understand his private.

Harris tried to answer, but his throat was squeezed shut. As if in an afterthought, the sergeant eased up on the pressure.

"Well, are you a coward?" he repeated.

"I . . . I'm an Assisian," Harris finally managed to choke out.

"Hell," the sergeant muttered, letting go of Harris' throat. "They got you crazies here, too? Was that what Sergeant Koppleman was trying to tell me about you?"

Harris rubbed his throat, trying to regain his breath. As the sergeant looked at him as he might an ant, Harris felt his anger rise. He wanted to do nothing more than punch the sergeant in the face, just one of many barbarians who demeaned his religion at best, persecuted them at worst. Time and time again throughout his life, he wanted to lash out—which was exactly what the Assisian Creed told him not to do.

He reverted to his catechism:

We are all God's children.
No one may cause harm to any other.
To do so is an assault upon God.

Slowly his anger faded as the sergeant stared at him. This man, this sergeant, only held authority over him by an act of man. Harris reminded himself that he answered to a higher being.

"How can a grown man be part of that sect?" the sergeant asked.

"We're not a sect," Harris muttered.

Sergeant Lin ignored the comment and asked, "You got family, Tayman?"

Surprised by the question, Harris stammered out, "Yes, Sergeant. My parents, brother, and two sisters. Back in Little Fork."

"So, Tayman, what are you going to do when the Wolvics come into your village, huh? When they want to kill your dad and brother, rape your mother and sisters? You've been given a weapon, you're there. Are you going to let them do that? To your family?"

"No."

"That's it? No? How're you gonna stop them? Shoot them?"

"No."

"Jesus Christ, Tayman. Then how? Talk them out of it?"

"Yes, Sergeant. I'm going to try and talk them out of it."

"Fuck, you are an idiot. Didn't you hear what happened to Brookstone?"

"Yes, Sergeant. I did."

When the 33 of them had been impressed into the militia, the Master Sergeant Koppleman had told them all about Brookstone, a small town only 20 klicks downriver. The Wolvics had leveled it, killing every man, woman, and child.

"And somehow you think you can talk these animals out of anything? Are you that dense?"

"No, Sergeant. I probably can't. But I'll have to try."

"And when that doesn't work? What then?"

"I would ask that they kill me instead."

The sergeant took half a step back in surprise, then his eyes narrowed, and he leaned back in. "They'll do that for sure. Right before they go ahead with the rest of your family. And for what? So, you can all meet up in heaven?"

"If there is a heaven, then I hope we would. If there isn't, then at least we lived our lives for the good here on Capernica."

Sergeant Lin's lip curled in disgust before he said, "I should just end your sorry excuse for a life. You're a hazard to the squad."

Harris stared back. If the sergeant went for his knife, he'd try and hold the man off. He'd probably fail, but he had to try.

"Tell you what. You finally fired your Brady up there. I take it you didn't hit anyone?"

"No, Sergeant. I aimed high."

"Can you keep firing? I mean, if we're in another firefight, will you fire your Brady, even if you don't try and hit anyone?"

Harris looked hard at the sergeant, trying to delve into the man's mind and figure out what he was trying to do. But it had been a simple question, and he couldn't see a moral trap.

What would St. Francis say?

He couldn't remember any reason why he couldn't fire the weapon. It may be the devil's tool, but it was only a tool.

"I can do that. I will do that."

"Then we'll do that. Maybe the Wolvic fuckdicks will target you instead of one of the others," the sergeant said. "You OK with that?"

"Yes, Sergeant. I'm OK with that," Harris said, suddenly relieved that he was still alive and the sergeant wasn't going to kill him.

Sergeant Lin turned and started back up the ridge. Harris stared at his back for a few long seconds, picked up his weapon from the dirt, then trudged after him.

Chapter 6

Harris had never been popular growing up, but at least he had been able to socialize with others in Little Fork. Now, he was persona non grata and, except for Lisa, was being ostracized. They branded him a coward. None of them knew anything about the military three days ago, but after a few hours of training, and now having been blooded in battle, they felt like accomplished soldiers. Safer d'Amay might have shit his trousers in fear, but he'd fought on. Harris, as they all now knew, hadn't even tried to hit one of the Wolvics.

It started with insults, then with shoves and trips. Sergeant Lin just watched and let it happen with the only admonition not to get too rough. They needed Harris as a target.

Harris barely slept through the night after taking the first watch. Every sound, no matter how slight, woke him, sure that someone was creeping up on him. He kept his hands clutched tight on his rifle. It had taken some internal debate, but he finally decided that giving someone a butt-stroke if they came after him didn't violate Assisian doctrine.

There was one thought running through his head for most of the night: desertion. He knew these woods, having spent most of his young life wandering the area around Little Fork. He was sure he could slip away, but to what end? As the master sergeant had warned him, the penalty for desertion was death, and that was a sure thing. He might die during the next battle, but then again, he might survive.

But if he deserted, his family might suffer. No, *would* suffer, and he couldn't put them through that. He didn't think the master sergeant was serious about punishing his family, but they would suffer the scorn and anger from the rest of the village. Then there was the fact that while Assisians believed in the sanctity of life, they also believed in secular law and order. Without it, humankind would fall into anarchy, and that would lead to widespread death and destruction. Capernica had accepted his family as colonists when other planets turned them away, and he owed a debt to the people. He was pretty sure he couldn't pay that debt as a soldier, but he certainly couldn't by running away.

Harris was tired but relieved when dawn finally lit the sky. At least, now he could see anyone coming. He sat to the side, eating his combat rats as others prepared food and wondered what the day would bring. They might be off on a village camping trip if it weren't for the far-off sounds of explosions reminding them of the war.

"You OK?" Lisa asked as she stood over him.

"I'm alive," Harris said.

"That's better than the alternative," she said with a laugh before moving on to sit with her battle-buddy.

There was still a dark stain in the dirt where his own battle-buddy had died. Just yesterday morning, Landon had been telling Harris that he was going to ask Babee Olivera to marry him when all this was over. Now, he was gone. Harris reached down and grabbed a handful of dirt and started spreading it over the bloodstain.

He only had it half-covered when Sergeant Lin broke the morning calm. "Listen up. We move in ten."

"What's going on," Johnjohn asked as people started gathering their gear.

"It's time for us to earn our pay, boys and girls," the sergeant said. "The Wolvics are on the move, and it looks like their next stop is your very own Little Fork."

Chapter 7

There was a renewed sense of purpose among the squad as they pushed to reach Little Fork. That was their home, not some unnamed ridgeline in the wilderness. Those were their families there. Harris shared that renewal of purpose. He wasn't sure what he'd do to protect his family from the Wolvics, but he did know he should be with them, especially if this marked the end.

He was tempted to pray for their safety as he pushed through the brush to reach the creek on the bottom of the cut, but the Assisians did not believe in prayer for personal intervention. To do so inferred that one person deserved more than another, and embedded in the Assisian canon was that all creatures were created equal, and all deserved God's love and compassion.

Even Wolvics, he tried to convince himself.

They pushed up the other side, fighting the thick vegetation with leaden legs and burning lungs, but no one slowed. If Sergeant Lin knew how close the Wolvics were, he wasn't sharing that intel, and all everyone could think of was to beat the enemy to the village. Harris wasn't the only one to sigh with relief when they crested Parker's Ridge. His legs were trembling, but below them were Crab Creek and the Tomiko Road. This was no time to stop.

En masse, the ten surviving militia and Sergeant Lin crashed pell-mell through the forest, their steps elongated with the gravity assist. Johnjohn fell in front of Harris to tumble down another 30 meters before he could stop himself, but he quickly jumped up, none-the-worse-for-wear beyond torn jeans and a bloody knee. Four minutes after cresting the ridge behind them, they stumbled out into the grassy creek bed and Tomiko Road.

"How far?" Sergeant Lin asked as he came out of the trees, chest bellowing.

Ivy pointed at a small stake pounded into the side of the road, "11.5" burned into it. "That's the distance to Tomiko, so Little Fork is just under four klicks that way," she said, shifting her arm to point downstream.

"OK, not far. Good. Look, the Wolvics are coming up the River Road, but I think we should be able to make it before them. The rest of the platoon, too, and we'll link up with them. But we can't just run blindly down the road. We've got to be on the alert in case they've got a screen going up this little river valley."

Harris wasn't sure they'd know about the Crab Creek Valley. Even if they did, this was the only road in, and it barely deserved the label. Unimproved, it was little more than a graded path that ran alongside the creek, crossing back and forth in a series of fords. If the Wolvics were coming, they'd be advancing up the River Highway, which ran along the east side of Green River, and was the main thoroughfare to Little Fork, built where Crab Creek flowed into the river.

"Morrisey, I want you on point. Olivera, you've got Tail End Charlie. We're going to double-time down the road, but keep your eyes peeled. We're not going to do anyone any good if we run up the ass end of a screening patrol."

When they'd left Little Fork two days ago, they'd marched in a column of twos, each person paired with their battle-buddy. With Landon dead, Harris no longer had a battle-buddy, and he wasn't sure where he was supposed to be. As the squad moved out, he slipped behind Ivy and Safer with Kath and Rainer behind him.

Harris tried to keep on the alert, watching for any sign of the enemy, but the high ground on the west side of the creek rose in a steep cliff, and if they were going to "run up the ass" of a Wolvic patrol, then the others would spot them first.

He was worried about his family, but he still couldn't help but wonder at how beautiful this place was. He barely remembered Xander, with its overpopulated cities, and this was a far cry from that. Dappled sunlight broke through the trees that arched and intertwined overhead, while the crystal-clear creek bubbled and gurgled as it made its way to the Green River.

Harris hadn't been on the Tomiko Road for half-a-dozen years, and most of the kilometer markers had long since disappeared, so, he wasn't exactly sure where they were until he saw the stanchions for First Bridge up ahead. There had never been a Second Bridge, as far as Harris knew, and there was no longer a First Bridge after it had been washed away in a spring flood a couple of years back. But while it crossed the deepest stretch of Crab Creek, that was still only knee-deep, so there had never been a strong impetus to rebuild it. A dozer had cut a simple depression in the meter-high bluff on the west side to give access to vehicles.

As one, the squad members perked up. They should be coming up on Old Lady Willowbee's place within ten minutes, then the village proper was right beyond that.

Johnjohn and Didi stepped into Crab Creek, pushed their way across, and started to continue before Sergeant Lin yelled out, "Morrisey and Donatelli, you two stop! What did I tell you about movement security?"

Johnjohn turned his head to look down the road, then back to the Sergeant. "But we didn't do any of that at the other fords," he protested.

"Which were what, all of ankle-deep?" the sergeant said as the next two entered the water. "Push out ten meters and cover the rest of us. We don't move out until the last one of us is across."

Johnjohn shrugged, but he and Didi split apart, then went down to one knee, eyes outboard. Georg and Bull crossed the creek, looked around in confusion until taking spots next to Johnjohn and Didi.

"No, you idiots! Dispersion!" Sergeant Lin shouted, splashing past Addad and Nok, knees lifting high.

Harris thought the sergeant was going overboard, but he wasn't going to say anything. He was right on Safer and Ivy's asses as they stepped into the creek, so he stopped for a moment to get some distance between them. When they'd gone about 3 meters, Harris followed, the cool of the water soothing to his tired feet.

Safer stopped midstream, then squatted. Harris didn't know what the guy was doing for a moment before it dawned on him. The guy had shit his pants the day before, and there was only so much he could have done up on the ridgeline to clean up. While the sergeant was bodily moving the others around to get them dispersed, Safer was taking the opportunity to get a quick rinse.

Harris didn't blame him, but the moment the sergeant turned around and spotted him, the NCO was going to take a chunk out of Safer's ass.

There was a whirring sound, almost like a giant hummingbird just as Safer slipped and went under. Harris lunged forward and caught the edge of the younger man's collar and hauled him up. The creek was turning red beside the limp body . . .

They're shooting as us!

More by instinct than anything else, Harris leaped backward, dragging Safer to the cover of one of the platiscrete stanchions. The whirring sound filled the ford, and Harris wondered how he could have confused the sound with that of a hummingbird. It was the sound of evil, of the devil himself.

"Are you OK?" he asked Safer, pulling his body up.

But Safer wasn't OK and never would be again. He'd been hit in the neck, shoulder, and jaw, three small holes that went completely through his body.

"What is that thing?" Ivy called out from where she was crouching behind the opposite stanchion, her face splattered with mud.

Almost immediately, the water around her erupted into tiny geysers. Ivy cried out in pain, then dragged her leg in behind the stanchion.

Harris knew he should stay behind his cover, but he couldn't help it. He eased his head around the corner of the stanchion to look across the creek. Two bodies—it looked like Georg and Didi—were motionless on the far bank. The rest were in the creek huddled up against the creek bluff. On the other side, almost invisible in the shadows, was a small, squat machine. Harris didn't need military service to recognize the SAAPU, the Semi-Autonomous Anti Personnel Unit. He might not know the exact model, but he'd watched enough holovids to know they were in deep trouble.

"Where's Lent! We need that goddamned vac," the sergeant shouted from where he was crouched with Johnjohn.

The "vac" was the VC-30, a scrambler, and Rainer had been carrying the squad's only one. Keeping as close as he could to the stanchion, Harris turned around . . . and there was Rainer, two or three meters away. He was on his back, glazed eyes staring at the sun while impossibly bright red blood spread across the dirt road. Harris could just see the muzzle of the vac peeking out from under his shoulder.

"I think . . ." Harris started, his voice barely squeaking out a sound. He gathered himself, then shouted out, "I think he's dead, Sergeant!"

"What about the vac?"

"It's under him."

"You've got to get it, Tayman. That's our only hope."

Get it? With that thing over there? Are you crazy?

"I don't have any cover, Sergeant."

"Shit! I should have known. Kim, can you see it?" he asked.

"I'm hit in the leg, Sergeant."

"I didn't ask you that. Can you see the vac?"

"I . . . no, I can't," she said in a miserable, scared voice.

Harris looked across to her, knowing that she could see Rainer, but she frowned, then pointed to her leg, before tilting her head telling him to go.

"Olivera, what about you?" the sergeant called out as another whir cut him short.

Harris risked a peek, but the others were still there. Above them on the far side, however, the SAAPU moved forward five meters, stopping in the middle of a patch of sunlight. A meter tall, it was a dull, military gray, but in the sun, there was almost an iridescence to the armor, and armor that made it all but impervious to the squad's weapons. None of their small arms could penetrate it, only the single scrambler, a weapon so pricey that they were parceled out like jewels. The scrambler round didn't exactly penetrate the armor, but rather created an intense, momentary field that would shut down the thing's electronic brain.

"Olivera?" the sergeant called out again.

"You there, Kath?" Harris asked.

There was no answer.

"Tayman, it's got to be you. Time to man the fuck up."

With a sinking feeling in the pit of his stomach, Harris knew the sergeant was right. The SAAPU had thousands of the hypervelocity darts, and it commanded the entire area. There was no way that they could sneak off in the creek or back the way they came without being in its line of fire. He wasn't sure if the SAAPU could cross the creek, so, he and Ivy might be safe as long as they didn't move, but the minute the thing moved down to the water's edge, the others had no chance.

He looked up at Rainer's body. It was so close, only two meters away, but it might as well be a hundred. The SAAPU would nail him as soon as he moved. If he had a rope with a hook or something, maybe he could drag Rainer closer, but as long as he was wishing, he might as well go all out and wish for a tank. He had no rope. He patted Safer down, but he didn't find anything of use.

Unless . . .

"Now, Tayman, before that thing comes down here," the sergeant asked.

"Don't be a fucking coward, Sparrow," Johnjohn shouted, using an old nickname that Harris despised. "Just do it."

Harris knew he had to act. Thinking it through would only drag things out until he couldn't move. He edged off his ass and into a crouch, making sure the stanchion still protected him.

"Sorry about this, Safer," he whispered.

He gave the body a shove into the current, yelling at the top of his lungs. He didn't know if the SAAPU reacted to sound, but at least it filled his body with adrenaline. Within a second, the water around Safer's body erupted as the SAAPU took it under fire. Without rational thought, Harris lunged out from behind the stanchion, dove stomach first flat on the ground, one arm reaching out to grab Ranier's utility harness. With strength born of fear, he yanked the body back over him, then twisted and dove for the cover of the stanchion.

It wasn't pretty. Rainer was a big man, and the two tumbled into the water as fire lanced through his side. Things were so confusing that he wasn't sure how he did it, only that he made it to the stanchion, breathing in huge gulps of air in panic.

He looked down at his side where blood was staining his issued camo blouse.

"You OK, Tayman?" the sergeant yelled.

Harris ignored him and fingered the hole in his side, head feeling dizzy, as he felt around to the back to the exit wound. He wasn't a student of anatomy, but he didn't think anything vital had been hit. It stung like heck, however.

I can't believe I did that, he thought, closing his eyes as the enormity of what he'd done sunk in.

"Tayman! What the hell's going on with you?"

"I'm OK, Sergeant," he finally answered.

"What about the vac?"

Good question.

Rainer was sprawled on his side, his body twisted. Harris started to reach out to flip the body over, then realized he'd just about exposed himself again. He took a deep breath, then slowly pulled Rainer in closer until he could grab the muzzle of the vac. It took some heavy jerking to get the sling to slide off his shoulder, but he had the vac in front of him. It looked undamaged.

"I think it's OK, Sergeant," Harris called. "Should I try and throw it to you?"

"Are you high? You'd probably drop it in the water. That, or overshoot us. No, you're going to fire the damned thing!"

"But . . ." Harris automatically started before trailing off.

He was about to say that he was a follower of St. Francis, and he couldn't kill. But that thing out there wasn't alive. Or was it? It had a type of consciousness, just not an organic one. Did that matter?

"No buts, Tayman. Listen up, and I'll tell you what to do."

Harris wasn't listening. He stared at the weapon in his hands. It was designed to "kill" enemy soldiers, the only difference being that the target soldiers were built by humans and "thought" by passing electrons through carbon nanotubes—much like their human creators, come to think about it.

Harris had never gotten too wrapped up with the philosophical discussions on what was life and what wasn't, but that was before he was sitting in Crab Creek with a scrambler and an enemy SAAPU trying to kill them. He tried to remember what stance the Assisians had embraced for artificial intelligences, but for the life of him, he couldn't recall it.

Ha! "For the life of me." Yeah, that's about right.

"Tayman! You still with me?"

"Yes, Sergeant. Sorry. I've been hit."

"Hit? Can you fire the vac?"

"I'm OK," he said, then mentally kicked himself.

He could have gotten out of having to fire the weapon with a lie. A little lie. Lying was not acceptable, but it was not as bad as taking a life.

"I can hear it coming closer!" Addad yelled, panic obvious.

"OK, Tayman, listen up. We don't have much time. You've got three rounds. That thing has defenses against scramblers, so you are going to use all three at once to overwhelm them. Look down on the right side of the stock. Do you see the selector lever?"

Harris turned the weapon over. There was a mechanical lever with three settings: "Safe," "Single," and "Volley."

"I see it."

"Don't flip it yet. See the trigger? It's a thumb trigger, just like on your Brady."

"Yes, Sergeant," he said, feeling nauseous.

"OK, Tayman. Easy-peasy. We're going to get up and fire on the thing. I'll give you a head's up, but as soon as you hear the first shot, you fire, OK?"

"But our weapons won't do anything to it," someone hissed, maybe Addad.

Harris didn't hear the full response, but it sounded like the Sergeant was saying they needed to give the SAAPU another target.

He looked over at Ivy, who immediately gave him a thumbs up.

"Are you still with me, Tayman?" the sergeant called out.

"Yes, Sergeant. I'm here."

"OK, OK. You're not going to have much time. The priority relevance programming won't take but an instant to realize that you're the threat, not us. You've got to fire off your rounds in that instant."

Which went against what they'd been taught over three days. They were supposed to fire their weapons after acquiring their target, and not to simply snap rounds downrange.

"How do I do that if I need to make sure to hit the thing?" Harris asked, realizing that by saying that, he'd already made up his mind and agreed to fire the weapon.

Others might argue, even the Assian Council, but the Wolvic SAAPU over there was not life in the strict sense of the term, and that was enough for him. He was going to try to take it out.

"The rounds will home in on it. You've just got to make sure you've got them in the cone."

A flurry of darts pinged off the stanchion, as if the SAAPU was listening in and was toying with them. Which made it seem more human.

Get that out of your mind. Just concentrate.

"I want you to take one last peek, Tayman. Just an instant. Get its location in your mind, OK?"

"Yes, sir. But when."

"Now, son. Do it now."

Harris took three deep breaths, whipped his head around the corner of the stanchion, then whipped it back before he considered what he'd seen.

Jonathan P. Brazee

"Sergeant, it's right above you. A couple of meters, max!"

"Fuck! No time! Tayman, flip the lever to "Volley and get ready! The rest of you, on my order, you fire on that fucking thing. Got it?"

Harris' hands trembled as he flipped the lever. This was it. Human reflexes against mechanical. How could he prevail?

"Tayman, get ready! Three . . . two . . . one!"

On one, the staccato of Bradlies, punctuated by the Sergeant's Bamberger, filled the ford. As if programmed, Harris rose, leveled the vac, and fired the volley, all in one smooth motion. There was a flash of blue light over the creek as the SAAPU intercepted the first round, then another just at the creek's edge, happening almost too quickly for the human eye to follow. The third flash was on the SAAPU itself—the third round had made it through the machine's defenses. Blue lightning enveloped the SAAPU, the single barrel spinning once before both the lightning and machine fell silent.

Harris hadn't moved. Addad had fallen back into the creek, the current starting to tug at the body, but the others had taken cover again.

Is it dead? Harris wondered.

He felt . . . he didn't know what he felt. Had he just killed? Or was it nothing more than turning off a light to go to sleep, turning off the autochef after the meal was produced?

"Tayman, get down!" the sergeant yelled.

Harris ignored him. He started across the creek, walking steadily against the pull of the current.

"Is he crazy?" Johnjohn asked as he reached the other side, then walked up the ramp.

There was a sharp smell of ionization in the normally pristine air, but the SAAPU didn't look damaged at all. It still looked like a deadly piece of war gear; its barrel hungry for a target. It didn't twitch, even when Harris reached out to touch it.

Is this what it feels like to kill someone?

A sense of pride, of victory, was taking over him. Part of him felt guilty about that. It was too close to the primeval

44

violence that lurked inside humans, tendencies that had to be suppressed. The other part of him wanted to tilt his head back and howl in exultation.

"Nice job, Tayman. You nailed the sucker," Sergeant Lin said.

Harris yanked his hand from the SAAPU and turned around. Sergeant Lin was standing at the edge of the creek, weapon at the ready. Johnjohn stood beside him, an odd expression on his face. Nok and Bull were dashing down the creek to recover Addad's body before it was swept away.

Across the creek, Ivy was struggling to stand up, and beyond her, much to Harris' surprise, Kath was slowly standing, refusing to meet his eyes. After a moment of relief that she was alive, he realized that she had refused to answer either the sergeant or him. She'd been too afraid, frozen by the danger. Anger swept through him, anger he had to fight before he said something he'd later regret.

The sergeant saved him. "Get McMoud ashore," he told Nok and Bull as they struggled with Addad's body. "We managed to survive this, but your village is still under threat, and our mission hasn't changed."

"Shouldn't we do something for . . . you know," Ivy said, limping across the creek.

"They'll be here later for that kind of thing. Right now, we've got to get going. Second Squad's already in place"

The sergeant walked up to Harris and poked at his side. He'd somehow forgotten that he'd been shot, but with the reminder, he was hit by a wave of pain that made him gasp.

"You going to be OK, Tayman? You going to make it the rest of the way?"

"Yes, Sergeant," he answered through gritted teeth.

Nothing was going to stop him from reaching his family.

Chapter 8

"Lynda!" Harris shouted as he caught a glimpse of his little sister being led away by Mrs. Rourke, the village's Pre-primary teacher. "Lynda, it's me!"

With her left hand clasped in the Smith girl's in front of her and her right in Finn Diamond's in back of her, she didn't hear him. They were too far from him to see much, but he could tell she was scared. He wanted nothing more than to rush over there, take her in his arms, and comfort her, telling her things would be alright . . . even if that was a lie. He'd commit that sin, however, if that's what it took to ease her fear.

"There's nothing back there for you," Sergeant Lin shouted. "The enemy's in front of us, so focus!"

Harris ignored the sergeant. Immediately upon reaching Little Fork, they had married up with Second Squad to form a hasty defense alongside the River Highway. There had been no time to try and find his family, and he'd been lucky to catch the glimpse of his sister amidst the chaos of the evacuation. He realized this might . . . probably would be the last time he'd see her, and he kept his eyes locked on the line of students until they rounded the All-Mart and disappeared from view.

"They'll be OK, Harris," Ivy said from beside him. "My dad's in charge of the evacuation."

Your dad's a drunk, he wanted to say.

With Safer dead, she didn't have a battle buddy, so Harris had positioned himself beside her. She was pale, looking like death warmed over. Her nanoinjector had taken care of the shock, but after reaching the village, her leg had stiffened up. The sergeant had slapped a pressure bandage over the wound, not bothering to remove her pants leg and with the dart still inside. Pumped full of happy juice, she swore her leg didn't hurt, but she still looked like a ghost.

A boom sounded from down the highway. All eyes swiveled to the south.

"Where do you think that is?" Ivy asked.

"I'm not sure. Maybe The Loft?" Harris guessed.

"Shit. I love that place. Fucking Wolvics."

If it was The Loft, a cozy restaurant and weekend music center, then the Wolvics were only four klicks away.

"Sarge, where are they now?" Johnjohn asked, voicing what they were all wondering.

"You just keep your eyes peeled, Morrisey," the sergeant said. "We'll know exactly where they are soon enough.

"All of you, check your clips and powerpacks again. Any powerpack less than 80 percent, switch out now."

"Sarge, I don't have another one, and I'm at 54 percent for this one," Johnjohn told him.

"Where the hell are your spares, Morrisey?"

"I think I dropped them back at the creek. I can run back and check."

"God save me from murdering my own soldiers," the sergeant said dramatically, then to Johnjohn, "No, there's no fucking time, shithead. Taymon, I know yours is over eighty percent. Give Morrisey one of your spares."

Harris opened his pouch, withdrew one of his two spares, and tossed it to Johnjohn. As if reminded of his presence, Sergeant Lin stood and walked over to him.

"I know all about that Assis bullshit you spouted, but this is for real now. This isn't some probe. That's your home there," he said, pointing behind them to the village. "And those are your people trying to get away. Do you understand that?"

"Yes, Sergeant."

"And . . . ?"

"I understand it."

"Fuck, you are dense. I mean, are you going to fight to save them?"

The others had been studiously ignoring the two, but now they turned to hear Harris' answer.

"I will not run, Sergeant."

"That's not what I asked you. Are you going to fight? Are you going to take your God-damned rifle and shoot the Wolvic sons-of-bitches that are about to come up that road?"

Harris opened his mouth, but nothing came out. The easiest course of action was to say he would, but aim to miss. He'd intended to say just that, but he lay there on his belly, his head craned up at the sergeant, his mouth gaping like a fish out of water.

No. No more lies.

"No, I won't, Sergeant," he said. "I will not kill a fellow human being."

"Piece of shit coward," Johnjohn said, and Ivy moved over another meter as if afraid of contamination.

Sergeant Lin stared at Harris for a long ten seconds, then deliberately unholstered his sidearm. He turned it over in his hand as if seeing it for the first time, then exploded into motion, too quick for Harris to react. He grabbed Harris by the back of the collar and yanked the taller man to his feet before pressing the barrel of his Colt-Clancy directly beneath Harris' ear.

"What if I tell you that I'm going to blow your brains out right here if you aren't going to fight," he said quietly, but with steel that cut like a knife.

The universe faded from Harris' consciousness. The only thing that existed with the muzzle digging into his jaw. He tried to pull back from the menace, but the sergeant was unbelievably strong, and his left hand kept Harris pinned.

"Well, Tayman? What's it going to be?"

The sergeant's voice was like the buzz of a gnat, annoying, but drowned out by the hard muzzle of the handgun.

"Well? Answer me!"

Harris' bladder started to release, and shame washed over him. With an effort, he clamped down to keep from pissing himself, then fought to turn his head to face the sergeant.

We're all going to die anyway in a few minutes. I'm not going out a killer or a liar.

"Shoot, if you have to," he said with as much scorn as he could manage . . . which wasn't much, to be honest. "I won't kill another being, even if you're so keen on killing those you are here and supposed to protect."

The sergeant's eyes were dead, like a snake's. There was no emotion in them. Around him, Harris could suddenly feel the tension from not only his squad, but Second Squad as well. He wanted to close his eyes, but he was going to make the sergeant look him dead on as he fired.

With a snort of disgust, the sergeant released his hold on Harris' collar. With legs like jelly, Harris fell to the dirt.

"I'm not wasting a single round on a worthless piece of shit like him," the sergeant announced to the rest of the squad as he re-holstered his Colt-Clancy. "Let the Wolvics finish him off.

"You, buddy up with Olivera," he told Ivy, who almost bolted to get away from Harris. "I'm not putting you with a battle buddy who doesn't have your back."

The sergeant went to John-John and Bull to check their position. He crouched behind them, checking their fields of fire before moving on to the next position, reminding them that the key was that their fields of fire were interlocking, theoretically creating a band of rounds that couldn't be breached.

Sergeant Lin didn't even glance at Harris as he went past him to the next position.

So much for taking out the SAAPU.

It might have been only half-an-hour ago, but what had transpired at First Bridge had been overtaken by events, those events being a large Wolvic force bearing down on the town. Harris understood that, but it still hurt.

A series of explosions walked up the road as his fellows yelled out and hugged the dirt. The explosions sounded sharper than usual and didn't produce the concussions they'd expected.

"Just EMP rounds," Sergeant Lin yelled. "They're prepping us."

Nervous laughter spread out in relief through the two squads. Most of them had no working wristcomps anymore, those having been knocked out the day before. Sergeant Lin and Third Squad's Corporal Synx had their meson comms with the master sergeant, but that was about it. The Wolvics were just wasting ammo.

49

"The skirmishers will be next," Corporal Synx yelled out. "As soon as they show themselves, fire!"

Despite everything, Harris perked up at the corporal's words and peered down the highway, looking for any sign. He'd heard much about the infamous Wolvic skirmishers, disk-mounted troops in the vanguard of larger formations, and they'd looked impressive in the images Sergeant Lin had shown them.

It didn't take long. Within a minute, a dozen black-armored skirmishers, perched on their disks ten meters over the ground, came gliding up the highway. Sergeant Lin had told them that this made the skirmishers vulnerable, and that they did this for show, to instill fear in poorly-trained soldiers. If the sergeant was right, then it was effective. Harris felt a tinge of panic and a strong desire to bolt back to safety. They were beyond human, the very forces of hell coming to punish the sinners.

"Fire!" Sergeant Lin shouted.

Rounds reached out from the squads, and the aura of invulnerability vanished as the skirmishers dropped to the ground for cover. One lurched and spun around, the disk oscillating wildly. Soldier and disk bounced hard on the side of the road, but the skirmisher got to his feet and scrambled for cover.

"Yeah!" Johnjohn shouted, getting to his knees, then dropping back down as the skirmishers took them under fire.

"That was just the show," Sergeant Lin shouted. "Now's the real thing."

Harris turned to look behind him and to his left, making sure he had a clear path. The two squads were arrayed alongside the levee that created the foundation for the River Highway where it turned in from Lookout Point. It gave them decent fields of fire down 200 meters of road to the bend, and negated the Wolvics' advantage in longer-range weapons. With the river at their backs, however, it was not defensible. Their mission was to take the vanguard under fire and make them deploy, then retrograde another hundred meters to the old McTarus factory, where the stone walls and roof would give them more protection from direct and indirect fire.

The initial firefight lasted less than a minute, the entire time Harris spent with his face in the dirt, waiting for the order to fall back to their secondary position. Neither skirmishers nor militia were gaining an immediate advantage, but the skirmishers were giving their first ranks of infantry time to move up. An automatic weapon opened fire, and the top of the levee began to disintegrate.

"Fall back, now!" Sergeant Lin screamed to be heard over the fire.

Lacey d'Lora in Third Squad was already moving, running in a blind panic along the top of the levee.

"Keep your head down!" Corporal Synx yelled, but too late.

Lacey's top third, everything from breast-level on up, disappeared in a cloud of pink mist just as she reached Harris.

Harris stared in shock as what was left of her tumbled down the rocks. He wiped away his face, his arm now red in Lacey's blood.

"You stupid fucks keep down!" Sergeant Lin shouted as he pulled Nok lower on the levee wall. She stumbled over the rough footing, almost bent in two, but she kept to her feet.

Harris slid down on his butt, keeping his head below the top edge of the levee. His mind was blank. No, not blank. It was whirling with so many emotions and inputs that nothing had a semblance of rational thought. He just wanted to live. A bloody chunk of what had been Lacey was in his path, and he just pushed it aside with his foot.

The levee had been constructed with the rocks blasted to make the cut through Lookout Point. They'd stood strong for over 30 years, but they made running difficult. Harris didn't care. He stood, then bolted down the levee wall, bounding from rock to rock. He passed Johnjohn and Bull, barely noticing them.

A blast sounded behind him. The Wolvics were employing their indirect fire. What kind, Harris didn't know, and he wasn't about to stop and see. His eyes were locked onto the old factory. With a last spurt of speed, he dove through the door, falling on his face on the cement floor. He lay there for a moment, gasping for breath.

"Of course, the coward makes it in first," Johnjohn said as he and Bull followed him in.

Harris was hyped, his adrenaline coursing, and he'd reached his breaking point. He turned to snap at Johnjohn to say he hadn't been a coward when he'd taken out the SAAPU, but Bull's sneer stopped him cold like a slap in the face. They were right. He'd run in fear, only thinking of himself, never of the others. He stared at his arms, still covered with Lacey's blood and shuddered.

As more piled through the door into the old factory, he got up off the floor and moved to the window, looking out. More of his fellow fighters were stumbling in. Ivy was holding her arm awkwardly, Sergeant Lin half holding her, half dragging her across the levee wall. He couldn't see if anyone else was down.

"Take up a firing position," Sergeant Lin ordered as he came through the door with Ivy. "Just make sure you have eyes on the road."

The McTarus factory had been built to help with the construction of Little Fork, back before there had been power or much of anything else. The bottom levels were the wheels and paddles that captured the power of the river's flow while the top four floors housed the machines necessary to create the village. With most of the building below the top of the levee, only the top two floors were above the highway. Sergeant Lin and Corporal Synx hadn't had time to assign fighting positions, so it was now up to each of them to find a spot. The factory had long been abandoned and stripped of whatever could be salvaged, including the windows, leaving the openings like dead eye sockets, and these were now to be their positions.

"Are you OK?" Harris asked Ivy.

"I've been hit again," she said, the right shoulder of her blouse stained dark red. "So, no, I'm not OK."

She brushed past him without another word to find a firing position. Shamed, he followed her up a floor. Most of the windows facing the highway were already taken, so he knelt beside one on the southwest-facing windows. He gave a quick peek out. He had a full view of the river, and the levee wall, then part of the highway. It was as good a position as any.

"Keep up the pressure," Corporal Synx was yelling, running from window to window. "This is your home. Are you going to let those Wolvic assholes take it from you?"

"No way. No fucking way!" Bull shouted.

Harris looked for Sergeant Lin, but he must have gone to the top floor. He gave a sigh of relief when rounds impacting on the outside of the building made him flinch.

I'm more worried about the sergeant than the Wolvics? he thought with a wry laugh.

"I'm glad you think this is funny, but you'd better be putting rounds downrange," Corporal Synx told him, taking a quick look out his window. "Hell, you don't have much of a shot from here. You make sure none of them start coming up along the riverbank, you hear? Drop anyone who tries."

Harris started to object, to explain that he wasn't going to target anyone, but then just gave up. What was the use?

At the bend, where they'd been positioned before—and where Lacey had been killed—Wolvics came into view. Two jumped over the top of the levee wall, then started to set up a crew-served gun of some sort. Harris looked around the room. Everyone was firing, but no one seemed to notice the two. He tried to form an image of the factory from above, and he realized that he might be the only one who could see them.

The two were hurriedly setting up the weapon, which looked to be a large-caliber machinegun. Harris looked down at his weapon, the charge and ammo load unchanged from when they reached Little Fork. He had yet to fire it today.

He cautiously poked the barrel through the window opening, keeping his head down. If he could see them, then they could see him. The crosshairs and gyro targeted the two, forcing the muzzle down and to the left. For a moment, Harris considered just letting go. He wasn't aiming his Brady, after all. It was doing it on its own. Just release the safety and press the trigger. Easy.

They were the ones invading. They were the ones killing the colonists.

"No!" he shouted, forcing the aim low and firing two rounds.

Both rounds impacted on the rock the two Wolvics were using as a base and cover. They ducked down, then one pointed right at Harris' window. The taller of the two swung the big gun around, and Harris barely had time to duck before rounds started hammering on the wall outside and coming through the window to impact on the far wall of the space, almost 20 meters away from Harris. Chunks of rock wall blasted off, showering Corporal Synx and making him dive out of the way.

The barrage lasted for a long twenty seconds before they shifted their fire, their noise lost in the general cacophony of the battle.

A hollow boom reverberated through the room, shaking it as dust fell from the ceiling.

"What happened up there?" Gif Leland asked, looking up in concern.

"You don't worry about that," Corporal Synx told him. "You just keep taking the bastards out."

Harris scooted back to the window, then slowly lifted his head. The two on the weapon were sending rounds down the highway. He couldn't tell if they were aiming at the factory or something else . . . that something else being the village. Movement caught his eye, and he raised his head slightly higher. Down along the edge of the river, six Wolvics were advancing, crouching to keep low. Where there were six now, he knew there would be more, and if they got into the factory, this fight was over.

His heart caught, and he half-raised his Brady. But still, he couldn't.

"Corporal!" he shouted out to report what he'd seen, but the man was on his comms.

A moment later the corporal shouted, "Hold on, people. We've got incoming air support."

Harris shifted to hug the southeast side of the window opening, watching over the river to the north. Within a few moments, he spotted it. A lone plane, hugging the water as it came to take on the Wolvics. It might even be the same one that had stopped the enemy probe the day before.

"Here it comes," he shouted.

Harris wasn't sure what one plane was going to be able to do, but he was sure glad to see it. He didn't even feel guilty for hoping the pilot would devastate the attackers.

As the plane came abreast of the factory, it popped up, then inverted to come back down, its gun chattering. The rocks making up the levee exploded in a mass of smoke and dust as the gun team and the six Wolvics below disappeared. One moment they were a threat, and the next, they were gone.

Harris erupted in a shout an instant before three missiles shot into the air. While it was probably hopeless, the pilot didn't even try to evade them. He kept firing, spewing death along the highway until the missiles connected, and his plane erupted in a ball of flame. Harris watched, mouth dropped open, as pieces of the plane showered the river, sending up plumes of water before the flow swallowed up all trace.

"He knew he couldn't survive," Harris whispered to himself, "yet still he came."

He shifted his gaze. There was no sign of the big machine gun, but there were bodies and body parts down along the river bank. One body was floating downstream.

"The plane is—" Harris started to say when his world exploded. A giant fist hit him in the chest and flung him against the back wall. Dust filled the air as he tried to make sense of what had just happened. The room, previously dim, was lighter now, the dust lit by direct sunlight. A good chunk of the wall was gone, as was part of the floor.

Groans reached him as he struggled to his feet.

Sergeant Lin burst into the room from the stairwell, taking stock. He knelt beside a face-down body in the middle of the room, blood already pooling on the ground. Harris couldn't see who it was, and he didn't want to.

The sergeant looked up and caught Harris' eye, then scowled and said, "Of course it would be the coward who makes it through."

"I . . . I . . ." but there was nothing. Harris didn't know what to say.

Ivy groaned and tried to sit, and the sergeant darted to her side. He gave her a quick scan, then shouted at Harris, "If you can't fucking fight, can you take Kim back to the aid station?"

The sergeant's voice sounded tinny and far away, and it took a moment for him to realize there was an "aid station," which was just the primary school manned by a few volunteers. It might not even be there anymore.

"Get your ass over here!" the sergeant shouted.

Harris dropped his rifle and staggered over to Ivy. Her arm was severed, blood pulsing in a weak stream from the ragged edges. He looked around for the rest of the arm, but he couldn't see anything. The sergeant slapped on a constricting pad, and like a living being, it molded itself around her stump, stopping the bleeding.

"Now, Tayman!" Sergeant Lin shouted before he dashed to the huge gap in the wall and fired outside. Answering fire reached into the factory.

"You OK?" he asked Ivy again, the second time with such a dumb question in ten minutes. This time, she was too far gone to answer.

He picked her up, surprised at how light she was. It couldn't just be the missing arm. He shifted her weight across his shoulders, wincing at the jolt of pain from his wounded side, then took the stairway down to the bottom floor, each moment expecting Wolvics to appear and cut them down. He made it to the river door unopposed, however. He took a couple of deep breaths, and pushed open the door.

When the factory was first made, the workforce had cut a smooth path that was more tunnel than open walkway along the river bank back to the rest of the village, saving them from lugging equipment and building supplies up three tall flights of stairs just to go back and forth. The sounds of the fight reached him, but the path was no different from the thousand other times he'd trod up and down it.

Ivy wasn't much of a burden, and he broke into a trot. He knew he might be hurting her, but she was out cold now, and he thought speed might be more important than being gentle. As the road sloped down into the village, the height of the levee wall gradually decreased, and by 250 meters, the path opened up to become a sidewalk alongside the road. Without the overhang, the sound of fighting was louder and more urgent. He passed "the Manor," the nickname given for the five spacious homes with views out to the river. Mr. Taliman's home was burning, a hole punched in its roof. The other four homes were untouched as of yet, not that Harris thought that would last.

He pushed the Manor from his thoughts. He had to get Ivy to the aid station.

"You still with me, Ivy?" he asked.

Nothing. She was a dead weight. He wanted to stop and check, but he couldn't do anything to help her either way, so he kept jogging down River Road, past the community center and the relay station to Orchid Lane and turned right, running up the short hill to the primary school.

He'd wondered why the aid station was in the school rather than the clinic, but the wire and red crosses made it clear. The school was a stand-alone building. The clinic was on the first floor of a shared building.

He went through the wire, and someone he didn't know, one of the volunteers who'd come to help, ran out and guided Harris to Ms. Tanaka's fifth-grade class. The children's desks had been rearranged so two could support 20mm plastic planks to make crude beds.

"Put her here," the volunteer said with authority.

Ivy looked pale as he lay her down.

"Is she going to live?" he asked the woman.

"I don't know. Let me see," she said, dismissing him before calling out, "Winston, I need your help over here."

Harris had been so focused on Ivy that he only now noticed that there were three people running a body scanner on someone else in the room, another person he didn't know, and out in the hallway, there was the bustle of others. Harris had thought that the village had been evacuated, but it was obvious that there were more than a few people left here, including outsiders.

Jonathan P. Brazee

He stumbled back out of Ms. Tanaka's room, the same room he'd spent a miserable year, his first in Little Fork. He couldn't have imagined back then what it would become right now.

"Harris! What are you doing here?"

Harris turned to be almost tackled by a welcomed sight.

"I should ask you that, Kate," he told his younger sister. "I thought you'd be gone."

"I wanted to help. When they brought in the people from Fox, I just couldn't leave them."

That answered who these people were. Fox was across the river, but it might as well have been on another planet, for all the folks in Little Fork considered it. If they were here, things must have been bad there, but why come when the Wolvics were marching on the town?

"Have you seen anyone else?" Kate asked.

"I saw Lynda leaving with the rest of the little ones, but that was not even half-an-hour ago."

"That's all? They were supposed to leave this morning. What happened?"

"I don't know, but look, Kate, you've got to get out of here. The Wolvics are right down the road."

She looked up and down the main hall, then said, "I don't know."

"I do. I've seen what happens. I just brought in Ivy Kim. I don't know if she's dead or alive. This is her blood," he said, holding out his hands. Hers and Lacey d'Lora's'."

"Ivy? Ivy Kim?" she asked, turning pale, reaching out to touch the blood on his arm. "I should help."

"Kate," he said, taking her by the shoulders. "You're fifteen. You're not a doctor. You need to leave. Get up into the caverns with the rest."

She looked unsure of herself, and he could see the emotions playing across her face.

"Go."

She took his hand and started pulling him to the door and said, "OK. Let's go. You need to come with me."

58

He let her lead him to the door and out of the building when something stopped him. The sound of fighting was close, too close.

"Why did you stop? You're right. We have to go!" she said, her voice rising.

The image of the lone pilot, flying a suicide mission, all to buy the militia and the town a few more minutes, flashed before him.

"I can't go with you," he told her. "You go."

"What do you mean?" she almost shrieked as she pulled on his arm, which made him wince in pain and double over. "You're hurt," she said, pushing against his side. "That's not Ivy's blood."

"I'm OK. You go," he said, tearing free of her grip and running down to River Road.

He blocked out her screams at him. He knew if he stopped, he wouldn't have the courage to go back to the factory.

His thoughts were a blur as he ran up River Road, past the Manor, and onto the path. A shell exploded behind him, but his mind was numb. With each step, he called himself a fool and asked why he was going back to that hell. It would have been so easy to take Kate and disappear into the hills, getting lost in one of the many caverns that laced the mountains, and hoping they'd be too much trouble for the Wolvics to dig out.

But something stronger kept him going, something he couldn't quite put his finger on. Honor? Maybe. Discipline? That was a laugh. Loyalty? Possibly. Whatever it was, he couldn't disobey the imperative it created in him.

Within a few minutes, he was inside the factory and climbing the stairs. The third floor, where he'd been before, was empty, at least of the living. Three bodies were up against the back wall. He didn't look to see who they were. The sounds of heavy fighting were above him, and that's where he had to go.

He climbed up the stairs, one careful step at a time until he was on the fourth floor, and he looked into a scene from hell. Rounds were punching through the walls, sending splinters of stone shooting into the space, yet Sergeant Lin and the others were standing steady, putting out an intense barrage of fire of their own.

This was humanity at its worst, on both sides, but the intensity on the faces of his fellow villagers shocked him. These were people he knew. Maria Augustini made ice cream, for goodness' sake, and now she was screaming in rage as she emptied her magazine.

Johnjohn was just in front of him, and he dropped back down to change magazines when he caught sight of Harris standing in the doorway.

"Hell, look who came back," he said with a sneer. "I lost that bet. I thought you'd desert."

Harris opened his mouth to protest, but nothing came out. Not that it mattered. Johnjohn was already back up to his window, firing out. Harris didn't know what to do. He knew he should have left with Kate—coming back served no purpose. He turned to look back down the stairwell when a blast took out part of the wall, showering him with tiny stone particles. His ears ringing, he turned back. Sunlight was streaming in through the hole where Johnjohn had been, lighting up the swirling dust and smoke.

Johnjohn was on his back, his right hand raised and waving feebly.

"Tayman!" Sergeant Lin shouted. "Pull him back out of the line of fire."

Harris automatically stepped forward, two rounds zipping past his head like angry wasps. He grabbed Johnjohn by the belt and dragged him back into the stairwell.

Johnjohn looked up at him, fear clouding his eyes. His mouth gaped open as he tried to say something, but nothing came out, and he caught Harris' arm in a vise-grip. Blood started to soak his fatigue blouse, but Harris was trapped looking at his left ear . . . or what had been his left ear. Only a small flap of cartilage was left.

"Help me," Johnjohn finally managed to get out.

"Just hold on," Harris said.

He looked back into the space to see what the sergeant wanted him to do, but the soldier was firing again.

"Help me, Harris," Johnjohn said again.

Harris couldn't help him. He wasn't a doctor. They were back at the . . .

And he knew what he had to do.

Johnjohn was twice Ivy's size, and Harris struggled to get him to his shoulder. Johnjohn cried out in pain, telling him to be careful, but he ignored the man. He had to get him back to the aid station.

The stairs were torture, each step opening the hole in his side. He almost went to his knees after the last step onto the bottom floor, but he managed to cross to the door, pushing it open.

The walkway was still clear. It wasn't easily visible from the highway above, and he doubted the Wolvics even knew it was there. He tottered into a slow trot, using their combined momentum to keep him going.

Johnjohn was semi-conscious, repeating "Oh, God, oh God, oh God."

His fellow militiaman was slipping, and Harris had to stop and hitch him higher on his shoulders, which caused the man to scream out in pain.

"Shut up, Johnjohn," Harris snapped, telling himself that he didn't want the approaching Wolvics to hear them. But he knew he was angry at the man, blaming him for . . . for everything. For getting bullied in Ms. Tanaka's class. For making Harris an outsider. For his sense of superiority over the last few days. For accusing him of being a coward.

And he knew that wasn't fair. The man was in pain, and he'd probably die. He didn't deserve Harris' ire.

"Sorry, Johnjohn," he muttered as he tottered forward again.

He couldn't run anymore, but he could walk. One step at a time.

Harris was mildly surprised when his feet turned up Orchid on their own accord. Wending through the wire, he made it to the front door, but he couldn't make it any farther, and no one came to help this time.

He dropped Johnjohn more abruptly than he'd intended, and the man cried out again.

"I need some help out here," Harris shouted, leaning against the door frame.

"Harris, what are you doing here," Doctor Akai asked, poking his head out of a window. "I thought you were fighting."

"It's Johnjohn. He needs help."

The youngest of the town's two doctors leaned out farther and saw Johnjohn, then said, "Oh, God. I'll be right there."

"Doc Akai's coming," Harris told Johnjohn. "You're going to make it."

He started to turn away. He could still join Kate. He'd done enough, bringing back Ivy and Johnjohn. They couldn't expect any more from him.

Before he could take a step, a strong arm grabbed his leg.

"Thanks, Harris," Johnjohn said, holding onto him. "I . . ."

Whatever he was going to say was left unspoken. He just looked at Harris for a moment, and then Doc Akai was there, running body scans. Johnjohn kept staring at Harris as he backed away, never saying a word.

Harris finally broke eye contact and turned, shuddering. Johnjohn freaked him out. But he was safe, if the Wolvics honored the red cross, and Harris had done enough. It was time to get away.

So, he was completely surprised when he turned left on River instead of right, toward the factory instead of out of town and into the hills.

What are you doing, Harris? he asked himself. *You've done enough.*

He couldn't fool himself, however. He knew he had to get back. His squad was still in the fight.

Without Johnjohn's weight bearing him down, he felt a surge of energy, and he was able to break into a run. The sounds of the fight were close, and instead of running along the sidewalk, he darted to the side into the yards of the Manor houses, jumping over debris. He felt terribly exposed, expecting to see the Wolvics marching down the road, and it was with a huge sigh of relief when he darted down and to the walkway back to the factory. With the overhang, he had some cover.

He'd made it half-way back when bodies rushed him, and his heart almost stopped, but it wasn't the Wolvics. Bull, Nok, and three of the others were rushing at him, panic in their eyes.

"Turn around," Nok yelled. "They've taken the factory."

"Where're the rest?" Harris asked, grabbing her by the shoulder as the others rushed past him.

"I don't know. Dead, I think," she said, trying to break free of his iron grip.

"You think? Did you see them?"

"No! But they were close, and there was no more time," she almost screamed, and with an adrenaline-fueled jerk, pulled free and chased after the others.

Harris hesitated. This was his out. No one could accuse him of being a coward now. He watched Nok disappear down the path, and he tried to will his feet to follow. But she hadn't been sure if the rest were dead, and he had to find out.

He slowed to a jog, all his senses on max alert. He could hear sounds coming from the road above, but they were muffled, and for all he knew, they could be echoes coming from farther back.

Harris reached the door, grabbed the handle, then hesitated. He could turn back now and run. No one would be the wiser. Instead, as if some higher force was in control of his body, he pushed open the door and entered the power room. It was no darker than it was when he'd left it such a short time ago, but it seemed more oppressive, more fraught with danger. He couldn't hear anyone inside, however, and he made his way past the surviving machines, relics of the pioneering past of Little Fork.

"We settled this town, not you," he muttered, heedless of the fact that his family had been in the fifth wave, long after Little Fork had been established.

He carefully made his way to the stairwell, ears straining to catch anything out of the ordinary. The outside battle still raged, but he compartmentalized that, muting the sounds as he focused on the inside of the factory.

The door to the second floor was closed. Harris put his ear against it, but he heard nothing. He debated taking a look, but decided that he didn't have the time, and he hurried up to the third floor taking two steps at once, wincing as his side protested.

The door to the third floor had been blasted away, leaving the stairwell exposed. Almost a third of the walls were gone, as were a couple of the structural columns, which caused the ceiling—and the fourth floor—to sink. Harris didn't care about the building. He needed to see if there was anyone left alive.

The same three bodies were still alongside the back wall. Blood had spread out more, but otherwise, they were unchanged. Harris didn't bother to look, afraid of who they might be. They were people he knew, but as long as he didn't see their faces, then it wasn't real.

He stepped closer to the blasted wall and stumbled on something soft. He caught his balance, then realized that he'd stepped on a body, or, rather, half of one. The Regular Army trousers identified Corporal Synx. Harris felt the gorge rise within him, and he had to fight to keep it down. Bile burned his throat.

This was all the evidence Harris needed to confirm the absolute stupidity of war. Corporal Synx was an outsider, a foreigner, yet he'd come to help save Little Fork, and now, he was dead. For what? So, the Wolvics could say they were in charge? So, they could wallow in the planet's productivity? It was a perversion of all that is good and right in the universe. If he'd ever doubted the Assisan teachings, this just verified the righteousness of it.

He quickly scanned the room. There might be another body or two in the rubble, but he was sure there was no one left alive. He spit, trying to clear the sourness from his mouth and started for the stairwell when a clatter from below stopped him in his tracks. He looked for someplace to duck behind, but there was nothing. At the last moment, he fell to the ground, face down.

He couldn't stop the tremor in his hands as he lay there, sure he'd be spotted. The feet stopped at the third floor, and he heard muffled voices. He couldn't make out the words, but he was sure they were Wolvic soldiers. A moment later, the group continued up the stairs.

Harris remained frozen, wishing he'd had his face turned to the stairs. He couldn't wait forever, so he slowly turned his head.

"Thank God," he whispered when he saw that the stairwell was empty.

He scrambled to his feet, and keeping as quiet as possible, he crept to it, ready to descend and hopefully make it to someplace safe. Looking up to see if the coast was clear, he was momentarily blinded by sunlight.

They're on the roof, he realized.

It made sense. They'd be security for the main force as they pushed into Little Fork. Sergeant Lin hadn't put anyone up there because they'd have no overhead cover, but the Wolvics didn't have to worry about that.

And that meant that the fourth floor might still be clear.

So, what? Get out of here, Harris.

But he had to know. If there was any chance someone was left alive . . .

Just a quick look. Ten seconds, max. Then, I'm outta here.

He bounded up the stairs, hugging the walls to minimize the chance that someone looking down from the roof would see him, burst into the fourth floor for a quick scan, and stopped dead in his tracks.

Like a scene plucked from a holo, Sergeant Lin was on the ground, covered in dust, his back up against what was left of the forward wall. Uniformly covered in gray, his eyes were stark white as he looked up at him.

Standing over the sergeant was a Wolvic soldier, his rifle leveled at him. His head started to turn at Harris' entrance, the muzzle of his weapon following.

Harris was moving before his mind realized what he was doing. He crossed the open ten meters in three strides, just as the Wolvic fired.

The first dart punctured Harris' left bicep, but the second was pulled high as the soldier backpedaled before Harris' fury. Harris hit the man in the chest, head down, shoulder first in a move that would warm the heart of any battleball coach. He drove the man backward and to the floor, landing hard on the man's sternum.

The man grunted in pain, and Harris pulled the rifle from his hands by the barrel, raised it, and swung it down with all his might, the stock smashing the side of the soldier's face, glancing off. Harris rose to his knees and swung again, smashing through the man's feeble attempts to ward off the blow, breaking his forearm and hitting him flush on the forehead. Full of righteous fury, angry at everything that had happened, angry at what he'd become, he raised the now broken weapon for one last blow to the whimpering soldier.

"No . . . please," the soldier begged, eyes wide in fear.

And Harris stopped the swing and threw the broken rifle across the room as if it had burned him.

"What am I doing?" he shouted, jumping back from the soldier, ashamed at what had come over him.

"You are killing a Wolvic," Sergeant Lin said from behind him. "Like a good soldier."

Harris turned around. The sergeant hadn't moved, and he seemed . . . *broken.*

"I never thought I'd see you again. Figured you'd have deserted."

"I was going to," Harris said. "Are you OK?" before mentally kicking himself for asking the same stupid question he'd asked Ivy—twice.

"I've been better," the sergeant said.

"Why are you still here? I mean, I saw the others leaving, and you said—"

"A change in our orders," Sergeant Lin said before a fit of coughing overtook him. Blood dribbled down his chin, turning the dust there red. He recovered his breath, then said, "The Air Force is on its way. The real one, not your Air Guard. We were told to keep the Wolvics out of your village and on the highway so they could stop them."

"But they're—"

"We failed. I told the others to get out, but I'm . . ." he said, dipping a chin to indicate his inert body.

He didn't look human, covered in dust. Harris didn't want to see him like that, so he looked back at the Wolvic soldier. The man hadn't moved, and his eyes were closed, but his chest was moving steadily up and down. Harris felt relief that he hadn't killed the guy, shame that he'd attacked him like a madman.

Shouting from right outside reached them. Harris edged to the hole in the wall and looked out. Not 15 meters away, a soldier was standing, shouting at him. No, not at him. At whoever was on the roof. The soldier listened, gave a thumbs up, then turned and moved out of sight.

Harris ducked down beside the sergeant and asked, "Why haven't they moved into Little Fork yet? There's no one to stop them."

"The Wolvics are deliberate bastards," the sergeant said, his voice reedy and faint. "Hear that humming out there? That's their armor. They'll bring it up before they make their push."

Which meant they might still have time, he realized.

"Can you move at all?"

Sergeant Lin managed to raise two fingers on his left hand, albeit shakily. He started to laugh, then started wheezing. Harris knew the man's time was running out. He didn't even contemplate leaving the sergeant. Kneeling beside the man, he took one of his hands, placed it over his neck, then reached between the sergeant's crotch with his other arm, wincing in pain. He'd somehow forgotten the dart that had passed through his bicep. With a heave, he stood, shifting the sergeant to his shoulders.

Sergeant Lin gasped, then asked, "Are you sure you want to do this, Tayman? I won't hold it against you."

Harris could barely hear the man, and he chose not to answer. He didn't want to be tempted.

There was a shuffling sound behind him, and Harris turned, the sergeant almost slipping off his shoulder. The Wolvic soldier was sitting up, a shaky hand holding a wicked-looking handgun.

"Stop!" he said. "You stop right now."

Harris fixated on the muzzle, which looked huge.

"I said stop. You put him down," the soldier ordered, his voice breaking.

"No."

"What? What do you mean, no?" he asked, his hand wavering more.

"I mean, no. I'm not putting him down. You do what you have to do, but I'm not going to let him die."

Harris deliberately turned around and started walking to the stairwell, expecting to be cut down at any second. A-few-steps-that-seemed-to-take-a-day-to-cover-later, he edged into the blasted well and took his first steps down.

"God, you've got balls," Sergeant Lin whispered before falling silent.

Step-by-step, Harris descended the stairs. He had nothing left if another Wolvic appeared, but the Gods of War—or maybe the Gods of Fools—smiled upon them, and he made it to the bottom floor safely. His adrenaline, which had been coursing through his body played out, and his strength began to fail again. He could feel a warm wetness flow down his side, and he knew his wound from . . . was it only an hour ago? . . . had opened up.

If he put the sergeant down, he was never going to get him back up, so he did the only thing he could do. He pushed through the door and staggered out. He had 250 meters of walkway, then another 150 or so to Orchid Lane.

"That's nothing," he told himself, grunting with each step.

Above him, just out of view, he could hear the Wolvics as they prepared for the final push into the village. From the sounds of it, that was going to kick off any moment. The Air Force wasn't going to save them. Harris was tempted just to sit down and let events unfold, but he'd seen the Wolvic soldier about to kill the helpless sergeant back at the factory, and he wasn't under any false assumption that they'd receive any mercy when they were inevitably discovered. He had to get Sergeant Lin to the aid station and that protective red cross. If the Wolvics would even honor that.

"Of course, they will," he grunted, heedless of the Wolvics just meters above him. "They have to."

Blood drenched his left arm, making his hold on the sergeant tenuous. Keeping him on his back became a balancing act, but like the man on the high-wire, a fall now would be fatal. He couldn't drop him.

And the walkway opened up. He stopped, blinking in confusion before he realized that he'd somehow made the 250 meters. Up ahead, just out of sight, was Orchid Lane. He started to move out to the road, his fuzzy brain barely registering a body on the road, then taking over at the last second and turning him to the left, toward the Manor houses. Just because the Wolvics hadn't kicked off their final assault didn't mean they didn't have the road under fire.

That lump was Nok, he saw. She'd made it down the walkway, only to be cut down in the middle of River Road. He shook his head, to clear it, and almost lost the sergeant.

"You still with me?" he asked.

There was no response.

Harris tottered over to the houses, moving behind the Foringelli's house. Each of the five houses had porches where the owners could sit and watch the river flow by. They weren't wide, but they offered a path for Harris, out of the road and line of fire. Taliman's house was still burning, and the heat almost drove him back, but with a burst of effort, he got past it. From there to the last house, it was surprisingly easy going, and he was soon standing alongside the Smith place, the last house in the Manor. Orchid Lane was kitty-corner to him, another 20 meters down and across River Road. It was so close; he could almost spit to it . . . if his mouth wasn't as dry as a desert.

Two people in white lab coats were standing in the front of the school, just behind the wire. One was placing a white flag with a red cross over the wire. Sweat was stinging his eyes, but he squinted. The man placing the flag was Doctor Akai, but he didn't recognize the other. It took a moment for what they were doing to sink in. They knew the village was going to be taken, and they were doing what they could to make sure the Wolvics knew it was a hospital.

A small drone was hovering in front of the two. The Wolvics knew what they were doing. The question was if they would honor convention.

The drone reminded him that he needed to move. There could be other drones that would spot him. He had to get the sergeant to safety.

Harris could hesitate, to catch his breath, but if he did, he'd never move again. With a grunt, he started running across the road. He made it half-way before the first round hit him in the knee, sending him sprawling. Chips of River Road spit around him as more rounds were fired. He lunged with his good leg to cover the sergeant, who was sprawled in a heap. Another round struck him high on the shoulder, the shock worse than the pain. His vision began to narrow as darkness fought for control.

"Just a little farther," a voice cut through the fog. Harris raised his head. Doc Akai and the other man were hugging the side of the Action Mart, out of the Wolvic's line of fire, but not venturing out. Just ten meters away.

The Wolvics had stopped firing, undoubtedly thinking he was dead. He felt dead. Numb, at least, which was probably a blessing. If he moved, however, he knew they'd open up again. Slowly moving his head, he looked back down River Road.

Three huge tanks were driving forward, one up and two back. Behind them, infantry was following. The assault on Little Creek had commenced.

Harris was not going to let the tanks crush the sergeant and him into a bloody stain on the road. He couldn't stand, but he had one good leg and one good arm. It was going to have to do. With a superhuman effort, he swung around and sat up, facing the sergeant. He grabbed the sergeant's collar, and with his good leg, pushed off. He moved less than a meter, but it was a start. He pushed twice more before the Wolvics noticed and took him under fire. Pieces of River Road hit him, then a round in his bad leg. Pain lanced through him, numb no more.

"You can do it," the sergeant said, urging him on. Harris had assumed the sergeant was dead, but those four words buttressed his will, and with a shout, he gave another push, then another before two more hammer blows took everything from him.

"I'm sorry," he started before hands grabbed him and pulled.

He tried to fight the Wolvics, but the voice said, "I've got you. I've got you, son."

It was the second doctor. Doctor Akai had Sergeant Lin, and the two were being dragged back to the aid station. Each step sent jolts of pain through him, but he didn't care. He was going to be safe.

A huge concussion swept over them, making the second doctor stumble. Harris wanted to cry out in rage, but his throat wasn't working. After everything, the Wolvics weren't honoring convention.

Doctor Akai and the new doctor stopped, mouths open as they looked up. More explosions sounded, and as Harris lay there, staring at the sky, a flight of six gunships flew directly overhead, their cannons chattering death.

"You get 'em, boys!" Doctor Akai shouted, jumping up and down and punching the air. He ran out to River Road and turned to watch as explosion followed explosion.

It took a while for it to sink in to Harris. The Air Force had arrived, and they were going to stop the Wolvic advance.

He turned his head. Sergeant Lin was beside him, eyes open.

"Are you OK?" Harris asked.

"You sure ask the stupidest questions, Tayman," the sergeant said with a wry smile.

"On the road, were you shot?"

"If I was, I couldn't feel it. Nothing below my chest. But you . . . you're all sorts of fucked-up."

"Did I screw up? Should we have stayed in the factory?" he asked in a hoarse whisper.

"We'd be dead if we were. You hear that shit going on?" the sergeant said, coughing.

"OK, let's see to you son," the doctor said, turning back to him and kneeling.

"Oh, hell," the doctor said, not waiting for an answer. "I need some help here," he shouted back to the aid station, not even scanning him.

Harris was vaguely aware that the doctor was doing something to him, but he wasn't sure what. He didn't even care. Snippets of what was going on broke through the fog, of being carried inside and placed on a table, of Doctor Akai describing the factory getting blown to bits and the pass at the bend being destroyed, cutting off the road.

He drifted in and out of consciousness, but when he heard the new doctor say, "I don't think we're going to be able to save him," his eyes snapped open, and he turned his head to where Sergeant Lin was on the next table.

But the doctors and several others were standing over him, covered in blood.

My blood, he realized.

"Brave young man," the new doctor said.

"Brave? He's a coward," Doctor Akai said. "You know, one of those Asissian pacifists. Won't fight."

"He's no coward," Sergeant Lin shouted.

Doctor Akai turned around and said, "Calm down, sergeant. I didn't mean anything. He's a nice enough kid, but they won't fight at all. I'm sorry about him, but . . ."

"He carried three of us to safety. Came back and fought a Wolvic to save me, and from what you say, it's gonna cost him his life. Like I said, he's no coward."

Doctor Akai frowned and turned back to the new doctor and asked, "Are you sure we can't do anything?"

"Maybe back in a Class A facility, but even then. No, I'm just surprised he's still with us. It won't be long now."

"Then I'm going to see to our sergeant here. He's not out of the woods, and the more we can do now, the better he'll be."

As Doctor Akai turned back to Sergeant Lin, the new doctor stood over Harris, one hand on his shoulder.

"Coward? I don't think so," he said gently.

"Coward" was just a word. Harris had kept to his moral code, and what more could be asked of anyone?

He slowly smiled and embraced the darkness.

Thanks for reading *Conscientious Objector*. I hope you enjoyed it. As always, I welcome a review on Amazon, Goodreads, or any other outlet. I hope you will read the other two books in the series, *Pogue* and *Retiree*. All three books are connected, but they are stand-alone reads.

If you would like updates on new books releases, news, or special offers, please consider signing up for my mailing list. Your email will not be sold, rented, or in any other way disseminated. If you are interested, please sign up at the link below:

http://eepurl.com/bnFSHH

Other Books by Jonathan Brazee

Call to Arms: Capernica
Conscientious Objector
POG
Veteran

The United Federation Marine Corps
Recruit
Sergeant
Lieutenant
Captain
Major
Lieutenant Colonel
Colonel
Commandant

Rebel (Set in the UFMC universe.)
Behind Enemy Lines (A UFMC Prequel)
The Accidental War (A Ryck Lysander Short Story Published in *BOB's Bar: Tales from the Multiverse*)

The United Federation Marine Corps' Lysander Twins
Legacy Marines

Esther's Story: Recon Marine
Noah's Story: Marine Tanker
Esther's Story: Special Duty
Blood United

Coda

Women of the United Federation Marines
Gladiator
Sniper
Corpsman

High Value Target (A Gracie Medicine Crow Short Story)
BOLO Mission (A Gracie Medicine Crow Short Story)
Weaponized Math (A Gracie Medicine Crow Novelette, Published in
The Expanding Universe 3, a 2017 Nebula Award Finalist)

The Navy of Humankind: Wasp Squadron
Fire Ant (2018 Nebula Award Finalist)
Crystals
Ace
Fortitude

Ghost Marines
Integration (2018 Dragon Award Finalist)
Unification
Fusion

The Return of the Marines Trilogy
The Few
The Proud
The Marines

The Al Anbar Chronicles: First Marine Expeditionary Force--Iraq
Prisoner of Fallujah
Combat Corpsman
Sniper

Werewolf of Marines
Werewolf of Marines: Semper Lycanus
Werewolf of Marines: Patria Lycanus
Werewolf of Marines: Pax Lycanus

To the Shores of Tripoli

Wererat

Darwin's Quest: The Search for the Ultimate Survivor

Venus: A Paleolithic Short Story

Duty

Semper Fidelis

Checkmate (Originally Published in The Expanding Universe 4)

The Bridge (Originally Published in the Expanding Universe 5)

Golden Ticket (Originally Published in Hope is Not a Strategy)

The Lost One (Originally Published in Negotiation)

THE BOHICA WARRIORS
(with Michael Anderle and C. J. Fawcett)
Reprobates
Degenerates
Redeemables

Thor

SEEDS OF WAR
(With Lawrence Schoen)
Invasion
Scorched Earth
Bitter Harvest

Non-Fiction

Exercise for a Longer Life

The Effects of Environmental Activism on the Yellowfin Tuna
Industry

Author Website
http://www.jonathanbrazee.com

Made in the USA
Coppell, TX
28 February 2020